Linda Lael Miller has made the Western frontier her own special place, and never more so than in this heartwarming new series that brings four women west to share an inheritance—2,500 acres of timber and high-country grassland called Primrose Creek.

In this wonderful new series, four cousins discover the dangers and the joys, the hardship and the beauty, of frontier life. And each, in her own way, finds a love that will last an eternity. Join the McQuarry women in a special celebration of the love, courage, and family ties that made the West great.

Four special women. Four extraordinary stories.

THE WOMEN OF
PRIMROSE CREEK

BRIDGET

CHRISTY

SKYE

MEGAN

Praise for Linda Lael Miller's bestselling series

SPRINGWATER SEASONS

"A DELIGHTFUL AND DELICIOUS MINISERIES. . . . *Rachel* will charm you, enchant you, delight you, and quite simply hook you. . . . *Miranda* is a sensual marriage-of-convenience tale guaranteed to warm your heart all the way down to your toes. . . . The warmth that spreads through *Jessica* is captivating. . . . The gentle beauty of the tales and the delightful, warmhearted characters bring a slice of Americana straight onto readers' 'keeper' shelves. Linda Lael Miller's miniseries is a gift to treasure." —*Romantic Times*

"This hopeful tale is . . . infused with the sensuality that Miller is known for." —*Booklist*

"All the books in this collection have the Linda Lael Miller touch." —*Affaire de Coeur*

"Nobody brings the folksiness of the Old West to life better than Linda Lael Miller." —*BookPage*

"Another warm, tender story from the ever-so-talented pen of one of this genre's all-time favorites." —*Rendezvous*

"Miller . . . create[s] a warm and cozy love story." —*Publishers Weekly*

Acclaim for Linda Lael Miller's irresistible novels of love in the Wild West

SPRINGWATER

"Heartwarming. . . . Linda Lael Miller captures not only the ambiance of a small Western town, but the need for love, companionship, and kindness that is within all of us. . . . *Springwater* is what Americana romance is all about."
                                                            —*Romantic Times*

"A heartwarming tale with adorable and endearing characters."
                                                            —*Rendezvous*

A SPRINGWATER CHRISTMAS

"A tender and beautiful story. . . . Christmas is the perfect time of year to return to Springwater Station and the unforgettable characters we've come to know and love. . . . Linda Lael Miller has once more given us a gift of love."
                                                            —*Romantic Times*

THE VOW

"The Wild West comes alive through the loving touch of Linda Lael Miller's gifted words. . . . Breathtaking. . . . A romantic masterpiece. This one is a keeper you'll want to take down and read again and again."
                                                            —*Rendezvous*

"A beautiful tale of love lost and regained. . . . A magical Western romance . . . that would be a masterpiece in any era."
                                                            —Amazon.com

Books by Linda Lael Miller

Banner O'Brien	Caroline and the Raider
Corbin's Fancy	Pirates
Memory's Embrace	Knights
My Darling Melissa	My Outlaw
Angelfire	The Vow
Desire and Destiny	Two Brothers
Fletcher's Woman	Springwater
Lauralee	Springwater Seasons series:
Moonfire	Rachel
Wanton Angel	Savannah
Willow	Miranda
Princess Annie	Jessica
The Legacy	A Springwater Christmas
Taming Charlotte	One Wish
Yankee Wife	The Women of Primrose Creek series:
Daniel's Bride	Bridget
Lily and the Major	Christy
Emma and the Outlaw	Skye

Linda Lael Miller

The Women
of Primrose Creek

Skye

SONNET BOOKS
New York London Toronto Sydney Singapore

This book is a work of fiction. Names, characters, places and incidents are products of the author's imagination or are used fictitiously. Any resemblance to actual events or locales or persons, living or dead, is entirely coincidental.

An *Original* Publication of POCKET BOOKS

A Sonnet Book published by
POCKET BOOKS, a division of Simon & Schuster Inc.
1230 Avenue of the Americas, New York, NY 10020

Copyright © 2000 by Linda Lael Miller

ISBN: 0-671-04246-7

First Sonnet Books printing July 2000

10 9 8 7 6 5 4 3 2 1

SONNET BOOKS and colophon are trademarks of Simon & Schuster Inc.

Cover art by Robert Hunt

Printed in the U.S.A.

In memory of Stevie Jo Wiley Clark.
If there are horses in heaven,
and surely there must be,
then you are racing the wind.

Skye

Prologue

∞

The first strains of "Lorena" swelled from Malcolm Hicks's fiddle like smoke from the charred hopes of six hundred thousand dead men, Union and Confederate alike, and all those who had watched in vain for their return. All else was quiet, there in the newly built Community Hall, with its wooden floor, sanded smooth and varnished to lend spring to the reels and glide to the waltzes. The dancers stood in respectful silence, some with tears in their eyes. A few kept a hand resting on their heart, but one or two had set their jaws, like mules balking on a lead line.

Jake Vigil was among the latter. When he was just seventeen, he'd made his way west from Missouri, on his own, and so considered himself neither Yank nor Rebel. The way he figured, it was a waste looking backward, most times, when the present and the future were all that mattered, but he also knew that sometimes a person didn't have a choice.

Just as he began edging toward the double doors of the hall, which stood open to an October night rimed in frost, his gaze snagged on Christy McQuarry Shaw, the woman who would have been his wife if she hadn't changed her mind at the altar a year before. Losing her that way, with pretty much the whole town looking on, had probably been the single greatest humiliation of his life, but now, having gotten some perspective on the matter, he knew that the marriage would have been a mistake for both of them.

Tonight, swollen with her first child and standing close to her husband, Zachary Shaw, their arms linked, Christy fairly shimmered with happiness. Jake smiled, perhaps a little sadly, just as the last notes of Malcolm's tune drifted away into the night, and turned to make his escape.

Almost immediately, he collided with a woman he had to strain to recognize, so different was she without her customary garb of trousers, hat, and shirt. Something leaped inside him right away when their eyes met. Hers were brown, alight with mischief and intelligence. Her hair was the color of polished mahogany and done up somehow at the back of her head, all loose and soft and shiny.

Skye McQuarry.

"I'm sorry," he said, grasping her shoulders to steady her. "I didn't mean—"

She smiled, and Jake let his hands drop to his sides, stung in some sweet, fundamental way, and retreated a step. "I know you didn't," she said, and Jake would have sworn the back of his neck was sweating.

He was still stunned and took her in again, in one dizzying visual gasp. She was delectable, with her womanly figure and perfect skin, and there was something downright magical in the way she smiled, sort of secret-like, as though she might be casting a spell that could never be broken.

Her dress was green, and the skirts rustled, even though she was standing still. Her collarbones showed, and part of her shoulders—those shoulders he had presumed to touch. Beyond all that lay the undiscovered landscape of her nature, and he sensed the almost infinite range of it, knew that merely getting to know her would be the work of a lifetime, an adventure filled with mystery and wonder, pleasure and pain.

He stepped back again, remembering Christy. Remembering Amanda.

"You're Bridget Qualtrough's kid sister," he said, that being the first coherent remark that came to his mind, and immediately felt stupid.

She laughed, glancing back over her shoulder once, as if pursued. The sound of her nervous joy made the pit of Jake's gut quiver in a way that Malcolm's skill with the fiddle never could have done. "I'm Bridget Qualtrough's sister, indeed. And I have a name of my own. It's Skye." She looked behind her again, and Jake caught sight of a scowling young soldier, watching both of them with narrowed eyes.

He wouldn't have believed the change in the girl if he hadn't been a witness to it himself. The Skye McQuarry he recalled was a quiet, shy lass, usually keeping her face hidden under the brim of an old hat. How could that little hoyden have transformed herself into this almost mythically beautiful young woman in the space of a few months? Well, however it had happened, he hadn't been the only one to take notice. The soldier—a corporal, he thought—was starting toward them.

Jake felt a surge of protective fury even before Skye spoke again, this time in a rather urgent whisper. "Please," she said. "Dance with me. Now." The dim light of the lanterns flickered in her hair, danced in her eyes, threw shadows across her breasts. He took her into his arms and began to imagine things no gentleman should.

He swallowed, flushed. "Is that man bothering you?" he asked.

Her smile was dazzling. Spring sunshine following a dark winter. "Not anymore," she said.

Jake shook his head once, dizzy. They were moving awkwardly; he supposed it could have been called dancing.

"I reckon I ought to get back to the mill," he said when he saw that the corporal had been deflected, at least for the time being.

She clung to his hand and the back of his upper arm. "You mustn't leave me just yet," she enjoined with a sort of cheerful desperation. "Corporal Shelby is a persistent man. He'll be back, pestering me again, if he sees you leave."

Her brother-in-law, Trace Qualtrough, certainly could have protected her adequately, as could Shaw, her cousin by marriage. Jake wondered briefly why she had turned to him instead, decided he was flattered, and put the question out of his mind. "All right," he said lamely, for he was no hand with women, and he never had been.

He reminded himself, in a sort of last-ditch effort, that the other three members of that troublesome family were lookers, like Skye, infamous for their stubbornness and pride and all but impossible to manage. While Jake had put his disappointment over losing Christy behind him—for the most part, anyhow—and bore no grudges, he was about as inclined to have truck with another McQuarry female as a snakebitten man would be to hand-feed a rattler. It worried him no little bit, the way this woman had set things to stirring inside him all of a sudden.

She'd noticed his underlying discomfort with the situation, that was plain by the pink in her cheeks, but she didn't show him any quarter. That, too, was a McQuarry trait. No, she simply squared those fine shoulders and stood her ground, figuratively speaking. "We have something in common, Mr. Vigil," she said as Malcolm began to fiddle up a lively melody, accompanied now by a prospector with a washboard and a lumberjack blowing into an empty jug. "Besides knowing Christy, I mean. I've been tracking that wild bay stallion up in the hills, and Trace tells me you have, too. Well, you might as well know—it's only fair and honorable to tell you—that I plan on getting to him first."

Jake sighed. The idea of holding this particular

woman in his arms, even for an innocent purpose, muddled his reason and filled him with a combination of anticipation and foreboding. He heard himself chuckle. *"You're* after the bay?" he marveled. "A little snippet of a thing like you? Why, you'll get yourself killed."

Her cheeks flamed, and her chin went up a notch. She stiffened a little, there in his arms, and his left hand went of its own accord to rest upon the small of her back, while the fingers of his right closed more tightly around hers. "I can ride as well as anybody in the state of Nevada," she said. "Man *or* woman, side-saddle or astride."

"Well, you ought to take up some womanly pursuits," he advised. "Maybe sewing—cooking—" His voice fell away. He'd forgotten, just for a moment, that Skye was, after all, a McQuarry.

He and Skye waltzed, while everyone else in the hall kicked up their heels in a lively square dance. Her eyes flashed as she looked up at him, not just with fury but with a bridled passion that roused still more strong and improper yearnings. "It just so happens," she said with a chill, "that I *can* sew and cook. I know how to tend children, too—I've been helping to raise my nephew, Noah, ever since he was born. Therefore, Mr. Vigil, you needn't worry yourself with regards to my aptitude for 'womanly pursuits.' "

He stared at her, dumbfounded. She'd always been just a kid to him, Bridget's sister, Christy's cousin. He couldn't think why he should care whether she was angry with him or not—he hadn't approached *her* this fine autumn evening, after all—but care he did, and it terrified him.

She heaved a sigh worthy of a stage actress. "There," she said, after scanning the milling crowd. "Corporal Shelby has left. I won't keep you any longer."

He didn't want to let her go. "Miss McQuarry?"

"What is it?" she asked, about to turn away.

"Stay away from that stallion."

Up went the chin. "Kindly do not order me about, Mr. Vigil," she said. "For one thing, it's rude. For another, it's a complete waste of time." With that, she turned on one delicate heel and swept away, into the flurry of calico and sateen, denim and homespun.

As Jake watched her go, it struck him that there must have been twenty men in that hall, apart from the pesky corporal, who would have given as many acres and a team of good horses for the privilege of sharing just one dance with such a woman. She had male kinfolk to look out for her. Why had she sought refuge with him, of all people?

While he was struggling with that question, another tune began, and he made for the doorway, lost in thought. All the laws of time and space and substance seemed to have been suspended; some dark and secret part of him began to open to the light. The process was painful, like the thawing of a frozen limb.

He was clear outside before he remembered her land, six-hundred-odd acres of prime timber and grassland, on the southwest bank of Primrose Creek. Skye, Bridget, Christy, and her sister, Megan, had inherited the large plot from their paternal grandfather, each one given an equal share. He nearly turned and went back.

He went over his contract with the railroad, too, as he walked aimlessly toward the mill, for the subject was never far from his mind, night or day. The deal was pivotal, and he'd staked everything he had on fulfilling it. Through a streak of hard luck, he'd lost a lot of his own timber to the random fires that plagued the area in the late summer, and much of the milling equipment he'd borrowed money to buy had either broken down or was yet to be delivered from San Francisco. It soured things, more than a little, to recall that he was a man with pressing problems—somehow, holding Skye McQuarry, he'd forgotten that for a little while, and in that blessed interval, he'd simply been a man.

Chapter

1

❧

Primrose Creek, Nevada
Spring 1869

She stood facing him, hands on her hips, elbows jutting, feet firmly planted, as though to sprout roots and become a part of the landscape, like the giant pine trees around them. Her brown eyes flashed beneath the limp brim of that silly leather hat of hers, and tendrils of dark hair, its considerable length clasped at her nape with a gewgaw of some sort, danced against her smooth cheeks. In that moment, for all that she stood barely taller than his collarbone, Skye McQuarry seemed every bit as intractable to Jake Vigil as the Sierras themselves.

The last time they'd met, months before at a dance in town, she'd been a mite more gracious. Now, in her unwelcoming presence, Jake, well over six feet and brawny after years of swinging axes and working one end of a cross-cut saw fourteen hours a day, felt strangely like a schoolboy, hauled up in front of the class for some misdeed. It made him furious; he, too, set his feet, and he leaned in until their noses were only inches apart. He would have backed off if he hadn't been desperate, and never gone near her again, but there it was. He was fresh out of choices, or soon would be.

"Now, you listen to me, Miss McQuarry," he rasped, putting just the slightest emphasis on *McQuarry*, since the name alone, to him at least, conveyed volumes about ornery females. "I made you a reasonable offer. If you're holding out for more just because of that little bit of gold you've been panning out of the creek, you're making a foolish mistake."

Skye tilted her chin upward and held her ground. She couldn't have been more than eighteen, and though she was pretty as a primrose, she showed no signs of wilting, either from the unusually hot May sunshine or from the heat of his temper. "And if *you* think you're going to strip my land of timber—for any price—*you* are the one who's mistaken!" Amazingly, she stopped for a breath. "These trees haven't stood here for hundreds of years, Mr. Vigil, just so you can come along and whittle them to slivers for fancy houses and railroad ties and scatter the very dust of their bones across the floors of saloons—"

Jake was at the far reaches of his patience. He'd already explained to this hardheaded little hoyden that the land was *choked* with Ponderosa pine and Douglas fir, among other species, that thinning them would merely leave room for the others to thrive. He closed his eyes and searched his thoughts for an argument he hadn't already raised.

She took advantage of the brief silence and rushed on. "Furthermore, these are *living things*—I won't allow you to murder them for money!"

They were standing in the middle of a small clearing—Skye's portion of an enviable bequest—with tender spring grass at their feet and Primrose Creek glittering in the sunlight as it tumbled past. In every direction, the timber seemed to go on and on, dense as the hairs on a horse's hide, skirting the Sierras in shades of blue and green. It was in that tenuous moment of reflective silence that Jake remembered his own lost timber and was inspired to take another tack.

"It's only May," he pointed out, "and we went all of April without rain." He jabbed a finger toward the thickest stand of timber, where the trees stood cheek-to-jowl, their roots intertwined, competing for soil and sun and water. It was a natural invitation to fire on a truly horrendous scale, and Jake had seen enough flaming mountainsides to last him until the third Sunday of Never. "What do you think is going to happen to those precious trees of yours if we get a lightning storm?"

She paled at that, and, though he supposed he should have taken some satisfaction in the response, he didn't. "I'll *tell* you what, Miss McQuarry," he went on furiously. "They'll pass the sparks from one to another like old maids spreading gossip over the back fence!"

Her mouth—it was a lovely, soft mouth, he noticed, and not for the first time, either—opened and promptly closed again. Then, in the next moment, her gaze narrowed, and her brows drew closer together. Her hands sprang back to her hips. If he hadn't known she was a McQuarry, her countenance would have given her away all on its own. "You're just trying to scare me," she accused.

"Ask Trace," Jake challenged. Trace Qualtrough, the first outsider brave enough to marry into the hornets' nest of McQuarry women, was Skye's brother-in-law, having taken her elder sister, Bridget, to wife. Damn, but that family was complicated; it gave Jake a headache just trying to sort them out. They were hellions, every one of them, that much was certain; two pairs of sisters, first cousins, and the best land in the countryside was deed to them, free and clear.

In point of fact, Bridget and Christy didn't always get along with each other, but a grievance with one was a grievance with them all, and Jake knew—hell, *everybody* knew—they would stand shoulder-to-shoulder, like their trees, against any challenge from an outsider.

As easily as that, Jake let Christy sneak into his mind. Christy, who, with her younger sister, Megan, owned the land on the other side of Primrose Creek. Beautiful, spirited Christy. A long-buried ache twisted in his heart, and, employing his considerable will, he quelled it, retreated into the familiar state of numbness he'd been cultivating ever since he lost her.

"I don't need to ask Trace," Skye said, wrenching him back from his reveries as swiftly as if she'd grabbed the back of his collar and yanked him onto the balls of his feet. "This is *my* land. Granddaddy left it to me, and *I* decide what happens here."

Jake heaved a great sigh. He'd already tried buying Bridget's timber rights, and Megan's, too, and neither of them had given him a definitive answer, one way or the other. He'd be damned if he'd approach Christy with any such request, even if it meant bankruptcy—and it just might, if he couldn't fulfill the deal with the railroad. Besides, the finest stands of trees grew on Skye's share of the tract.

He was way behind schedule, and although he had modest holdings of his own, he'd already harvested the best stands of timber, those that hadn't burned the previous summer. To cut any more before the trees had time to come back would be plain stupid; despite appearances to the contrary, the resources of the West were not inexhaustible, and Jake knew it.

He heaved a great sigh. "I never should have wasted my breath trying to reason with a—with a—"

Skye raised one delicate eyebrow. "With a woman?" she asked softly. Dangerously. No doubt, she was still bristling from their conversation at the dance, when he'd suggested she leave off chasing the stallion and turn her mind to more feminine pursuits, and she'd taken offense at the remark. Neither of them had caught the bay, as it happened, but Jake figured she hadn't given up on the idea any more than he had.

"With a McQuarry!" Jake snapped. He wanted to give his temper free rein and bellow like a bull, but he knew he couldn't afford the indulgence. He had to win this argument, and soon. The fact that it seemed impossible only made him more determined.

Her very expressive mouth curved into a smile that

made Jake want to kiss her and, at one and the same time, turn right around and head for his horse. Damn if she wasn't even more confusing, even more hog-headed, than her cousin Christy, and that was saying something. "If that's supposed to be an insult, you'll have to do better. I'm *proud* of my name."

He looked around, maybe a little wildly, at the empty clearing. He couldn't remember when he'd been more exasperated with anybody, man or woman. "What are you going to use to build with, if you refuse to cut your precious trees?" It was a gamble; she had house-room at Trace and Bridget's place, everybody knew that, and as a single woman, she might elect to live right there until she married. On the other hand, she was who she was, a McQuarry female, and her people were an independent lot, making and following rules of their own. She'd probably live in a chicken coop if she took a notion.

For all of that, he could see that her confidence had ebbed again, the way it had when he mentioned the possibility of fire. Perhaps she was envisioning vast tracts of timber reduced to charred stumps and wisps of smoke in a matter of hours, as he was.

"I've got gold," she said. "I mean to buy lumber. To build my house, I mean."

Jake grinned without humor. He set his hands on his hips again, mirroring her stance; there wasn't another lumber yard within three hundred miles, and they both knew it. "Suppose I don't want to sell?" he inquired. He was being mulish, for sure and certain, but he couldn't seem to help himself. Something about this complicated woman set his nerves to singing, and not only was the music downright unsettling, but he felt compelled to dance to it.

Color surged up Skye's neck to pulse, apricot pink, beneath her high cheekbones. Jake felt a swift, grinding ache somewhere deep inside. "That's ridiculous," she cried. "Selling lumber is your business!"

"Exactly. And *I* decide when and if I'm willing to sell. Just like you."

From the look in her eyes, she wanted to kick him in the shins, but she must have found it within herself to forbear, for Jake remained unbruised. At least, on the outside. "You're doing this because you have a grudge against my cousin," she said, that obstinate chin jutting way out. "Christy married someone else, and you're taking it out on *me*."

Her words sent such a shock jolting through him that she might as well have struck him with a closed fist. The sensation was immediately, and mercifully, followed by a sort of thrumming numbness. "I don't do business that way," he insisted, but he'd taken too long to reply. He could see that by the narrowing of those brown eyes.

"Don't you?" she countered, folding her arms, and turned her back on him, big as life. He couldn't recall the last time someone had dared to do that.

He watched her in helpless irritation for several moments, then spun around, stormed over to his horse, a gray and white stallion he'd dubbed Trojan, and mounted. "You know where to find me," he said, and then he headed for town.

*   *   *

Skye waited until she was sure Jake Vigil was well out of sight before letting down her guard. With the back of one hand, she dashed at the tears of fury and frustration clinging to her cheeks. Maybe he was right, and she was being unreasonable, she thought. Maybe, by refusing to sell him so much as a twig of the timber growing on her land, she was punishing him for loving Christy the way he had.

The way he surely still did. She hadn't missed the way he'd reacted to the mention of her cousin.

Skye heaved a sigh and glanced up at the sun, the way someone else might have consulted a pocket watch. She'd best stop standing here and get on home; she'd promised Bridget she'd look after Noah and the babies while she and Trace went to town to pick up a load of supplies, and after that, she and her cousin Megan planned to gather wildflowers to press in their remembrance books. No sense standing around mooning over a man who would never see her as anything more than an obstacle between him and six hundred and twenty-five acres of prime timber.

She took one last, long look around at her land, where she planned to build a little cabin all her own, along with a good barn, and make a life for herself. She'd been saving the money she'd made panning gold, and pretty soon she'd be able to put up her buildings, buy a mare in foal from Trace and Bridget, and start a ranch all her own. The bay stallion, once she roped him in, would give distinction to her brand.

Just a week before, she'd nearly captured the exquisite bay stallion, wild as a storm wind, up near the tree line, but he was wily, and, in the end, he'd managed to elude her. That hadn't dimmed her determination to bring him in, though; she was set on the plan, and there would be no going back.

Trace and Zachary had promised to help with the building, and others would pitch in, too, Primrose Creek being that kind of town, but what good was a lot of willing labor without boards to make walls and floors and ceilings?

Head down, thoughts racing far ahead, like willful children, Skye started back toward Bridget and Trace's place, following the edge of the creek the way she always did. She had a room of her own with them, but the Qualtrough family was growing rapidly, and it wouldn't be long until things got real crowded. Besides, she couldn't help wanting to *begin* doing something real, something that was her own. As things stood, she was merely marking time, waiting for something, *anything,* to happen.

Within a few minutes, Skye rounded a curve in the creek, and her sister and brother-in-law's holdings came into view. The structure, fashioned of hewn logs, was large and sturdy, built to last. The door stood open to the fresh spring air, welcoming. Her six-year-old nephew, Noah, was running in circles in the front yard, whooping and hollering like a Paiute on the warpath, and Bridget immediately appeared on the threshold, smiling and wiping flour-covered hands on a blue-and-white checked apron.

Bridget was a beauty, with her fair tresses, perfect skin, and cornflower blue eyes. She was a small woman, and she looked deceptively delicate, even fragile. Skye had seen her face down Indians, bears, and the Ladies Aid Society, all without turning a hair.

"Did I just see Jake Vigil ride up the bank on the other side of the creek?" she asked. As her son raced past, she reached out and snagged him by the shirt collar. "Merciful heavens, Noah," she said good-naturedly, "that will be enough. Try being a *quiet* Indian."

Skye shaded her eyes with one hand. "He wants to cut down my timber," she said, as if that were an answer to her sister's inquiry.

Bridget sighed. "And you refused."

"Of course I did," Skye retorted, a little impatiently perhaps.

Bridget set her hands on her hips. "Why?"

For a moment, Skye couldn't recall what her reasoning had been—being near Jake always addled her—but then it all came back to her, like a flash flood racing through a dry creekbed. "He means to raze every tree on my land to the ground, that's why."

"Nonsense," Bridget scoffed. Like the rest of the McQuarrys, Bridget was never hesitant to express a differing opinion. "Jake's a very intelligent man, and he wouldn't do any such thing."

Skye had heard about the way some of the mining companies were ravaging the countryside, down Virginia City way and in other parts of the state, too. Why would the lumber industry be any kinder? "In any case, I told him no. And do you know how he responded?"

Her sister waited, no doubt to indicate that indeed she didn't have the first idea.

"He won't sell me the lumber I need for my house and barn. Even though I have cash money to pay him!"

Bridget looked pleasantly impatient; she cocked her head to one side and studied her sister with amusement. "Sounds to me like you two have reached a standoff. Both of you are plain stubborn, and that's a fact."

Skye felt color thump beneath the skin covering her cheekbones. "If you feel that way, why don't you sell him some of *your* timber?"

"Maybe I will. I haven't decided the matter."

Before Skye was forced to answer, Trace came whistling around the corner of the house, leading a team of two bay mares hitched to the family buckboard. The wagon rattled and jostled behind them.

Noah raced toward his stepfather. "You're going to town!" he crowed. "Can I go? Can I go?"

Trace ruffled the boy's gleaming brown hair and crouched to meet his eyes. He was as devoted a father to Noah, his late and best friend Mitch's child, as he was to the twins Bridget had borne him just the year before. Gideon and Rebecca were their names, and they were sunny toddlers now, with fat little legs and ready smiles. "Well, now," he said very thoughtfully in a confidential tone of voice, rubbing his chin as he pondered the situation, "I was kind of counting on you to look out for the womenfolk while I'm gone. Your Aunt Skye and little Rebecca, I mean. And then there's Miss Christy and Miss Megan, over there across the creek." He paused, sighed at the sheer magnitude of the task. Skye noticed he didn't include Caney Blue, the forthright black woman who ran the cousins' household; even Noah wouldn't have believed *she* needed a caretaker. "Gideon isn't quite big enough to handle the job, you know. I mean, suppose something happens that only you could take care of?"

Noah's small chest swelled with pride. He saw the babies as his special charge, and now that they were ambulatory and usually heading in two directions at once, he liked to keep an eye on them. *Just the way I always looked after him,* Skye thought with a small, sad smile. He was growing up so fast, Noah was. Before she knew it, he'd be a grown man, leading a life of his own, maybe even riding away for good. It made her heart ache to think of that.

"I'll watch out for the whole passel of 'em," the little boy said staunchly.

Trace did a creditable job of hiding a smile, though Skye saw it plainly, lurking in his eyes. "I'd appreciate that," he said with a grave nod of his blond head. "You and I, we'll make our own trip to town tomorrow morning," he finished. "No women allowed."

Noah beamed. "No women," he confirmed.

"What are you teaching that boy?" Bridget demanded, but there was a note in her voice that sounded suspiciously like laughter.

Trace rose easily to his feet. "Never you mind," he told his wife, grinning and mussing Noah's hair once again. As if it wasn't trouble enough keeping that child tidy. "We had some things to discuss, Noah and I. Personal stuff."

"Man-to-man," said Noah.

Bridget smiled and shook her head as she reached back to untie her apron. Trace's gaze followed the rise of her shapely breasts with a glint of admiration, and something as tangible as heat lightning passed between them.

Skye averted her eyes. She loved her sister better than anyone else in the world—she might not have survived all the grief they'd endured back in Virginia if not for Bridget, not to mention the long journey west that followed, but there were times, all the same, when she envied her a little. It seemed to Skye that Bridget had everything: a handsome, dedicated husband; three healthy, beautiful children; a house and land and horses. Although women were denied the vote and men could legally lay claim to any property their brides brought into a marriage, Bridget remained the sole owner of the six hundred and twenty-five acres she'd inherited from Granddaddy, and she often bought and sold livestock on her signature alone. Trace had an interest in the horses, of course, and in the investments the two of them made together, but he let Bridget tend to her own affairs. The two of them were partners in the truest sense of the word.

"We won't be long," Bridget promised when Skye joined her in the cool, shadowy interior of the house. The babies were in Noah's room, asleep in the little railed beds Trace had built for them, but they'd be awake soon enough, rambunctious as ever. "Is there anything you'd like us to bring back?"

Skye smiled ruefully. "A few wagonloads of lumber, perhaps?"

Bridget laughed and shook her head, draping her good shawl over her shoulders. She had crocheted the piece over the winter and liked to wear it because it made her feel dressed up. "I'm afraid you're going to have to give in and part with some of those trees," she said. "At least enough to provide logs for a cabin and some kind of shed."

Even that seemed like a travesty to Skye, who loved every pine and fir, every twig and branch on her property, but she gave a slight, rueful nod all the same. She longed for a home of her own, and besides, she suspected that Bridget was expecting another baby, even though she hadn't said anything to that effect.

Very soon, Skye knew, she would become a burden. An image of herself as a maiden aunt, scrawny and terse and disappointed, made her shiver.

Bridget laid a hand on her shoulder. "Brew yourself some tea, if the twins leave you time. That will make you feel better."

Tea was the balm for most every ailment and strife, as far as Bridget was concerned. Skye nodded again, managed a slight smile, and went to the door, where she and Noah stood waving until Bridget and Trace and their wagon had rattled across the creek, up the bank, and off toward town.

Noah resumed his chief-on-the-warpath game and promptly woke the twins. Wails came from the children's bedroom, shared with their older brother, and Skye rushed to fetch them, one in each arm.

Gideon and Rebecca were golden, blue-eyed babies, good-natured and intelligent. Being just up from their naps, however, they were both wet and fitful.

Skye snatched up two clean diapers and carried her niece and nephew outside, where she laid them down in the soft, sweet grass growing by the creek, beneath her favorite aspen tree, and changed them. They were more comfortable after that, and thus more cheerful, and they sat crowing and gurgling in the shade while their young aunt washed her hands at the stream.

She was sitting cross-legged on the ground, tickling their noses with blades of grass and delighting in their amusement, when Megan came splashing across the creek, riding her small brown-and-white pinto mare, Speckles. A slender, vibrantly energetic redhead, Megan was Skye's confidant, and the two of them, the children of feuding brothers, had all but grown up together back in Virginia on their grandparents' prosperous farm. Unlike Bridget and Christy, who got along most of the time but rarely sought out each other's company—and that alone was an improvement, considering the way they'd scrapped as children—Megan and Skye were best friends as well as cousins. The two of them often panned for gold together, and Megan had used her share of the proceeds to buy Speckles.

Letting the mare's reins dangle, Megan plopped down in the grass and hoisted Gideon onto her lap.

"I had to get away," she confided in a dramatic whisper, as though her elder sister might hear her from way over there, on the other side of the water, up the hill and inside the house Trace and Zachary and their friends had made of an old Indian lodge with a room added on just for Megan. "Christy's in a pet." Megan brushed a wisp of copper-penny hair back from her forehead, and her green eyes sparkled with mingled love and irritation. "I declare, ever since she lost her waist, she's been impossible. We'll all be glad when that baby comes." Christy and Zachary's first child was due soon, any day, in fact, and while Skye knew they were both thrilled, it was also true that pregnancy didn't seem to do a lot for Christy's disposition. Zachary was the only one who could really manage her, and he'd been away a lot lately, with a posse, trying to track down whoever was robbing the freight wagons and stagecoaches between Virginia City and Primrose Creek.

"Bridget was like that," Skye confided. "Cranky, I mean. Last time she was expecting. It'll pass."

Megan sighed heavily. "I suppose," she said, and then lay back on the cushiony ground and held Gideon up with both hands, causing him to chortle with slobbery good cheer. "She still insists that I go to normal school and earn my teaching certificate so I can always have 'security.'" Rebecca, wanting to share in her brother's adventures, tugged at Megan's sleeve until she got a turn, too. "Why can't Christy understand that things are different now that we're finally safe, the four of us?" She paused and sighed in a typically theatrical manner. "I've grown up and changed my mind about a lot of things. I want to be a stage actress—that's so much more exciting, don't you think, than teaching school?"

They often commiserated, Skye and Megan, being great friends; sometimes Bridget was the object of their frustration, but more often it was Christy. Skye felt especially charitable toward her elder cousin that day, though in truth it worried her a little, for she seemed to know Megan less and less these days. The rest of the family thought her fascination with the stage would pass, but Skye feared it wouldn't.

"She wants you to have a good life, that's all. What's so terrible about going to normal school, anyway? If you get tired of performing, you'll have that to fall back on."

Megan sat up, sprigs of grass caught in her gleaming hair, and held Rebecca on her lap, while Skye held Gideon. Noah, meanwhile, climbed deftly into the lower limbs of a nearby tree. "I don't want to learn another thing," she said in a familiar tone of determination. "At least, not about reading and writing and arithmetic. I want to travel all over the world, acting in plays, wearing splendid, sweeping gowns of velvet and silk, with hoods and tassels, and then come back to Primrose Creek, build a grand house on my share of the land, and live out the rest of my days in glorious notoriety." She lowered her voice. " 'She was once an actress,' people will say. I might even write my memoirs."

"Don't you want a husband?" Skye asked, though

the question was rhetorical because she knew the answer. Skye had business interests of her own to pursue, of course, but she craved a home and a family too and found it hard to comprehend that Megan had decided upon an entirely different path, especially since the two of them had wanted the same things for most of their lives. Skye got a lonely feeling just thinking of the changes in her closest friend.

"Perhaps," Megan relented, though grudgingly, "but not for a long, long time. He'd have to be older, with a great deal of money. An admirer, maybe, from my days on the stage."

Skye smiled. Megan was fond of Caleb Strand, a good-looking, dark-haired young man, employed as a sawyer with Jake Vigil's timber company, but he was only one of several suitors, and Megan treated all of them with affectionate disinterest. "What about your property? Surely you don't want to leave it." The McQuarrys were Irish at their roots, and love of the land was a part of them, body and spirit, like the penchant for horses and the willingness to put up a fight when one was called for.

Megan flushed slightly and brushed Rebecca's downy blond curls with her chin. "It'll be here when I get back, I reckon," she said. Her spring-green eyes, inherited from their beautiful grandmother, turned somber. "What about you, Skye? You'd like to marry, I know you would. And you could have a husband like that"—she snapped her fingers for emphasis—"if you weren't mooning over Jake Vigil all the time."

That morning's encounter with Mr. Vigil had all

but convinced Skye that what she'd thought was love for him had probably been a mere infatuation. Still, trying not to think about him was like trying not to breathe, not to let her heart beat. Knowing she'd idealized him, in the privacy of her thoughts since that night he'd rescued her at the dance, from a mere and fallible man into some kind of noble personage didn't lessen the strength of her emotions at all. "I'm not doing any such thing," she protested.

Megan merely smiled.

"I'm not," Skye insisted. But she was—wasn't she? Great Zeus and Jupiter, she wasn't sure of much of anything anymore.

"Oh, for pity's sake," Megan said. "Why don't you just rope him in and hog-tie him and be done with it? He's surely over his feelings for Christy by now. After all, it's been more than a year."

To Megan, and usually to Skye, too, a year was just shy of forever. That was one of the reasons Megan resisted going away to normal school and Skye wanted to start *living* like a grown woman. After all, she was eighteen. Lots of women had several children by that age.

Skye sighed. "That's just the trouble. I'm not so sure he *is* over her. The way he talks, *McQuarry* is another word for *obstinate*."

Megan shrugged. In the town of Primrose Creek, the male population far outnumbered the female, and a pretty young woman could have her pick of husbands. Megan had often pointed out that fact to Skye, forever trying to play the matchmaker. "I don't suppose you noticed," she said, "but Mr. Kincaid was quite taken with you." Megan had introduced her to the shy lumberjack, a newcomer to Primrose Creek, after church the Sunday before. "You could do worse, you know. He's thirty, and his teeth are excellent. You did notice his teeth?"

Skye giggled. "You make him sound like a horse up for auction. How are his feet? Maybe I should get him by the shin and lift one up, just to make sure he's really sturdy."

"Good teeth are not to be sneezed at," Megan said.

"I should hope not," Skye agreed.

Megan laughed and pretended to strike her a blow to the shoulder. This started a rough-and-tumble free-for-all, and soon all of them, babies, Noah, Megan, and Skye, were engaged in a lively mock wrestling match.

"Lord-a-mercy," boomed a familiar female voice, and everyone stopped to look up at Caney Blue. "What is all this carryin' on about?" the tall woman demanded, her dark eyes flashing with good humor. Caney had worked for the McQuarry family as a free woman, back in Virginia, along with her late husband, Titus. When Christy and Megan traveled west to claim their shares of the inheritance, Caney accompanied them. She'd been with them ever since, although she had plans to marry one Mr. Malcolm Hicks one day soon. Although obviously fond of her, Mr. Hicks had proven himself to be a hard man to wrestle down.

"Is Christy still in a snit?" Megan asked, getting to

her feet. She was holding Rebecca with an easy grace that said she would be a good mother one day, whether she thought so at present or not. "I'm not going home until she's over it, if she is."

"She's laborin' to push out that baby," Caney said. "I was hopin' Trace would be around, so I could send him out lookin' for the marshal. It ain't gonna be long."

"Trace is in town," Skye said.

"Zounds!" Megan gasped at almost the same time, and her face went so pale that all her freckles seemed to pop out on little springs. "I'll go and fetch him right this moment!" With that, she thrust little Rebecca at Skye, gathered up Speckles' reins, and mounted in a single smooth motion. All of Gideon McQuarry's grand-daughters were accomplished horsewomen. He'd seen to that, teaching them all to ride as soon as they could cling to a saddle horn.

Before anyone could even say good-bye, Megan and the mare were splashing across the creek and up the opposite bank, disappearing into the trees.

"Is there anything I can do?" Skye asked quietly of Caney. Instinctively, she'd gathered the twins and Noah close to her skirts, as though there were a storm approaching.

"You just say some prayers," Caney replied, unruf-fled. "I'll head on back. I reckon she'll be wanting me close by, Miss Christy will."

Skye nodded. Her throat felt thick, and she wanted to weep, though her emotions were rooted in happi-ness, not sorrow. To her, the birth of a child was the greatest possible miracle; she'd imagined herself bearing Mr. Vigil's babies a thousand times, for all the good pretending did. Well, it was time she got over that foolishness, wasn't it, and moved on.

"You'll send word if you need something?"

Caney was already headed back across the rustic footbridge Trace had constructed by binding several logs together to span the creek. "You'll hear me holler out if I do," she said.

Jake Vigil stood in his great, elaborate, empty house, gazing out the window at the naked flower gardens and trying to work out what had gone wrong between himself and Skye McQuarry. He was shy, it was true, but he was normally a persuasive man, able to make others see reason, even if they tended toward the hot-headed side, the way she did.

The faintest, most grudging of smiles curved his mouth as he remembered Skye standing there before him, arms akimbo, guarding her patch of ground. She was young, but she was pretty, and she was nubile. He remembered clearly how beautiful, how downright womanly, she'd been that night last fall at the dance, and because of that, he was able to see past her shapeless clothes and sloppy hat. Getting by her willful nature would take a little more doing.

They were at an impasse, he and the lovely Miss McQuarry. Sooner or later, someone would have to give in, and it damned well wasn't going to be him. One way or the other, he'd get what he wanted—with just one notable exception, he always had.

If he couldn't persuade Skye to sell him the timber

rights he needed, he was bound to lose everything. He thrust a hand through his hair. It wouldn't be the first time he'd started over; at thirty-four years of age, Jake had taken his share of hard knocks and then some, and he knew he could survive just about anything. That didn't mean he relished the idea.

After some time had passed, he turned from the window and sank into the richly upholstered leather chair behind his broad mahogany desk. He tilted his head back and closed his eyes, thinking about Christy McQuarry—now Mrs. Zachary Shaw. The image of her had kept him awake nights for the better part of three months, and he'd consumed a river of whiskey in a vain effort to put her out of his mind. Now, all of a sudden, he couldn't quite recall what she looked like. His thoughts kept straying back to Skye, with her chestnut hair and flashing, intelligent brown eyes. She was infuriating; that was why he couldn't get her out of his mind, he decided. She reminded him a little of Amanda.

Amanda. Now, there was a lady he would just as soon never think of again. The last time he'd seen her, she'd shot him in the shoulder with a derringer and left him to bleed to death. Though she'd taken the opportunity to clean out his cash box before leaving, of course.

He smiled again. He sure did know how to pick his women. First Amanda, trouble on two very shapely legs but good at pretense, and after her, Christy, who'd lured him to the altar and then abandoned him there to take up with Zachary Shaw. His smile faded. He'd made up his mind on that rainy, dismal occasion of his thwarted marriage that he'd guard his heart from then on and content himself with the attentions of the sporting ladies, over at the Golden Garter and Diamond Lil's, and he meant to abide by the decision.

Whether he wanted to or not.

*Y*ou could marry her," Malcolm Hicks said, sounding just as calm as if he'd suggested a sensible course of action. "Miss Skye, I mean."

Jake leaned against the framework of his office door, one arm braced at shoulder level, one thumb pressed against his chin. It was a stance he often assumed when he was flummoxed—which was more and more often, it seemed. His gaze sliced to Hicks, who was behind the desk, going over a ledger book. "I'd sooner court a prickly cactus than that woman. Besides, she probably wouldn't have me."

Malcolm wiped his pen thoughtfully and then laid it down on the blotter. A black man, born a slave on some steamy plantation in Georgia, he'd managed to get himself educated by hook and by crook, and because Caney Blue had come along and set about courting him first thing, he considered himself an expert on matters of the heart. "You're not only a damn fool," he said easily, "you're blind, too. That girl thinks you pull the moon behind you on a string. Everybody knows it but you."

A fist clenched around Jake's stomach, eased off again. He wanted to believe Malcolm, and, at one and the same time, he *didn't* want to. "She's a McQuarry," he said, as though that put the whole matter to rest. For him it did, to a large degree, though he could already tell that Malcolm wasn't going to accommodate him by agreeing.

Malcolm smiled and took up his pen again, pretending to ruminate. "That she surely is. They're thoroughbreds, them McQuarry women, and that's a fact. Miss Skye's strong and proud—she marries a weak man, she's going to be downright miserable to the end of her days, and so is he. Now, on the other hand, if she were to marry a fine, substantial feller such as you—"

"Forget it," Jake snapped. He was fresh out of patience, having used up a fair amount earlier in the day in the skirmish with that little troublemaker. He thrust himself away from the door frame. Away from the thought of being married to Skye McQuarry, with her lively intelligence, her fierce determination, her womanly body, and all the enticing mysteries of her spirit. He pointed to the open ledger. "You just keep your mind on the books. And while you're at it, find me a way to meet those notes of mine without supplying ten thousand railroad ties first."

Malcolm's smile went dark, a shadow falling across cold ground. "Ain't no way to do that," he said.

Jake sighed and left the room. He'd go back to the mill and work until his muscles hurt enough to take his thoughts off this new, strange soreness in the region of his heart, or better yet, maybe he'd take another crack at finding that bay stallion.

Skye lay on her belly in the high grass blanketing the ridge, watching as the magnificent stallion stood, head high, mane dancing against his sleek neck. He was long-legged and solid through the chest, built to outrun the wind. She smiled, but a little sadly. It was almost a travesty to capture such a splendid animal and break him to ride. Provided, of course, that he *could* be caught. Sometimes, watching him, Skye thought he wasn't real at all but an illusion, the mirage of a dream.

He raised his head and turned toward her, probably catching her scent on the breeze. For a long moment, they simply gazed at each other. Then, offering a loud whinny, as if in friendly challenge, he turned and loped away, disappearing into a tree-lined draw like a spirit.

Skye lingered there, in the spot where she'd crushed the grass, for a long while after he'd gone. It was something of a shock when she came to herself and realized that she'd stopped thinking about the stallion at some point, and Jake Vigil had sneaked into her mind instead.

She rolled over onto her back and gazed up at a blue and cloudless sky. She oughtn't to tarry. Christy had given birth to a baby boy the night before, and her husband, Zachary, still hadn't returned. Skye had promised to spell Caney and Megan for a while and sit with Christy and the new baby.

It would be hours until nightfall, but the moon was visible, transparent as cheesecloth, and she wondered if there would be any use in wishing on it. She'd already tried talking to stars, all to no avail. Jake might want the timber growing on her land, but beyond that, he'd probably never given her a thought.

She sighed, plucked a blade of grass, and clasped it lightly between her teeth. She supposed she could trade the timber for a wedding ring and hope Jake would come to love her in time, as such men, in such marriages, often came to love their wives, and vice versa, but the mere idea chafed her pride raw. It would be bad enough if he accepted such a proposal; if he were to turn her down, she'd be too mortified to set foot in the town of Primrose Creek ever again.

The sound of a wagon, echoing from below, distracted her from her musings; she sat up and turned in the opposite direction, squinting to make out the team of mules and the rig, lumbering along the narrow trail. A load of freight, probably bound for the general store or Mr. Vigil's lumber mill. He was forever sending to San Francisco or Denver or even Chicago for some fancy piece of equipment.

Skye blinked. She could make out Mr. Harriman's bulky shape, there in the wagon box, the reins clasped in his meaty hands. Beside him, a little boy sat clutching the hard board seat, white-knuckled, his brown hair gleaming in the sun. Even from far away, she could tell that the child was skinny and pale, and an ache of sympathy burrowed deep into an inner wall of her heart.

Poor little fellow. He seemed scared to death.

Frowning, Skye got to her feet, shook out her hopelessly rumpled homespun skirts, and headed for her cousin's house, which stood on a rise almost directly across the creek from Bridget and Trace's place. The Shaws' home, sporting a new roof and glass windows, not to mention wood floors and four separate and spacious rooms, in an area where rustic log cabins were the rule, was widely admired.

When she arrived, the front door was ajar, and although Caney wasn't visible, Skye could hear her inside, singing an old spiritual in that rich, melodic voice of hers. If Caney didn't marry Malcolm Hicks— which she fully intended to do—she might have made her living performing on a stage, as Megan wanted to do.

Skye tapped at the door frame and stepped inside. Caney was standing at the cookstove, with its gleaming chrome trim, stirring something savory in a pot. She smiled in greeting.

"Well, now, Miss Skye, you are a welcome sight."

Skye glanced uneasily toward the entrance to Christy and Zachary's room. "How is she?"

Caney sighed. "Pinin' something fierce, that girl, sure that Mr. Zachary won't be coming back to her, ever. Won't even name that baby boy."

"Where's Megan?" Skye asked. She was always half afraid, these days, of hearing that her cousin had taken to the road, in search of fame and adventure on the boards.

Caney flung her hands out wide and let them slap against her sides. "Heaven only knows. That girl's gonna get herself a reputation if she don't stop traipsin' to and fro the way she does. Always dreamin' and carryin' on like she's somebody out of one of them Shakespeare plays. Ophelia, she calls herself, or Lady Macbeth. I declare that chile gets too much sun."

Skye smiled. Megan did love to play a part, even if she was the only one in the show.

"Caney?" came a voice from the main bedroom. "Is that Zachary out there?"

Skye and Caney exchanged glances.

"No, miss," Caney called back. "It's your cousin Skye, come to sit with you awhile and admire that sweet boy-child of yours."

"Oh," Christy responded, plainly disappointed. Then, with an effort at cheer, she added, "Come in. Perhaps Caney wouldn't mind brewing us some tea before she goes to town."

Caney gestured for Skye to enter her cousin's room and then reached for the tea kettle.

Christy was propped up in bed, her dark hair spilling in ribbons and tangles of silk over the pillows at her back and down over her shoulders and breasts. Always fair-skinned, Christy was alarmingly pale now, and there was a look in her gray eyes that made Skye want to ride out and find Zachary Shaw herself, then skin him alive for being gone at a time like this in the first place. The new baby, an impossibly tiny bundle, lay in the curve of her arm, swaddled in a bright yellow blanket that Bridget had knitted during the winter.

"Let me see," Skye pleaded good-naturedly, stepping close to the bed.

Proudly, Christy turned back a fold of the blanket to reveal a dark-haired infant, contentedly sleeping. "Isn't he wonderful?" she whispered.

Skye drew up a chair and sat down. Her nod was a sincere one. "He's very fine indeed," she agreed. "Has he a name?" She knew he hadn't, but she hoped that raising the subject might turn Christy's thoughts in a more constructive direction.

Christy's face clouded, and, very gently, she covered the baby's head again. "We always argued about that, Zachary and I," she said, and gazed wistfully toward the window, as though she saw an angel hovering there, waiting to lead her home to heaven. "We'd settled on Elizabeth for a girl. If we had a son instead, I wanted to call him Zachary, of course. But my husband insists a boy ought to have a name all to himself, and not one he has to share with his father—"

"Christy," Skye interrupted, reaching out to squeeze her cousin's slender hand. It felt cool, even chilled. "Zachary's all right, you know. If anything had happened to him, someone would have come to tell us."

Christy sniffled. "I'm behaving like a hysterical fool, aren't I?"

Skye smiled. "No. You've had a baby, and you want your husband at your side; there's nothing wrong with that. But you'll make yourself sick if you worry too much."

"I can't seem to collect myself," Christy fretted. Then her deep gray eyes searched Skye's face. "We lost so many loved ones, didn't we? You and Bridget and Megan and me. Sometimes it seemed that the dying would never stop—" She paused, blinked back tears of panic. "You don't think fate would be so unkind—?"

Skye shook her head. "No. I'm sure Zachary will be back any time now. Then the two of you can add a brand-new name to the family Bible. Would you like me to bring it over?" The ancient, much-prized volume was in Bridget's keeping, but it belonged to the four of them, and Skye knew that every birth and marriage was faithfully inscribed, all the way back to the first owner, a young Irish immigrant named Robert McQuarry, who had fought in the Revolutionary War and subsequently received a land grant from General George Washington himself. So, too, were deaths, of course, although fortunately there had been none of those since the four surviving McQuarrys had reached Primrose Creek.

Christy's expression changed slightly at the mention of the McQuarry Bible. She averted her eyes for a moment, then met Skye's gaze squarely. "Yes," she said. "Yes, do bring the Bible, please." She sighed, relaxed a little, then became fretful again, though less so. "I should be up out of this bed. I don't care what the doctors say—it can't be good to lie about like an invalid."

Skye suspected it was Christy's worry that was keeping her abed rather than any medical necessity. That indeed it would be the best thing for her cousin to get up, dress, and get some fresh air and sunshine. "I could fetch Bridget if you like," she said, all innocence. "You know, to look after you——"

Christy's color rose encouragingly, and a certain fire snapped in her gray eyes. "Don't you dare," she said with quiet ferocity. "I have enough to contend with, without her lecturing me." The cousins, while no longer the sworn enemies they'd once been, still tended to bristle a bit at any suggestion of one needing the other's help. Lately, though, it almost seemed as though they were in collusion about something, keeping an uneasy secret.

"Here, then," Skye said, hiding a smile as she stood and extended her arms. "Let me hold that second cousin of mine while you get up. Just don't move too quickly."

Christy surrendered the infant, somewhat reluctantly, but when Skye left the room with the baby in her arms, she could hear the other woman walking around in the bedroom.

"How did you do that?" Caney asked, seeming a little miffed that someone else had succeeded where she'd failed. "I've been tryin' to roust that girl all morning."

Skye smiled and sat down in a rocking chair facing the fireplace. Caney had a tray in her hands; she'd been about to serve tea in the bedroom. Now, she set it down on a sturdy little table within Skye's reach. "I threatened to go and get Bridget," she whispered in reply.

Caney laughed, low and soft. "I always maintained you was a clever girl," she said. "Panning for gold, mind you. Savin' up your money. Makin' your plans, bold as a man. I surely never seen the likes of this family."

The baby was a warm, sweet-scented parcel, and Skye felt a pang, turning back the blanket and gazing down into that tiny face. For a moment, for just the merest, most fleeting moment, she allowed herself to pretend that she and Jake were married, and the child was her own. Jacob, she'd have him christened, but they'd call him by his middle name, so as not to confuse him with his father . . .

"What thoughts are goin' through that mind of yours just now?" Caney asked with her particular brand of rough tenderness. She was reaching back to untie the laces of her apron, bent on going to town to meet with Mr. Hicks, no doubt. "You got a look in your eye that reminds me of your old granddaddy."

Skye must have blushed a little; her face felt warm. She watched as Caney poured her tea, something she wouldn't ordinarily have done, except that Skye's hands were full. "I guess I was just making a wish," she said in a small voice.

Caney patted her on top of the head, just as she used to do when Skye was little, getting underfoot in the kitchen or the laundry room on the family farm back home. "You'll have your day, child," she said. "You'll have your day. And right soon, I reckon."

It was then that Christy came out of the bedroom,

clad in a faded-rose morning gown. Her gleaming dark hair trailed down her back, but she had brushed the tresses to a high shine, and there was a spark of spirit in her eyes.

"Well, look at you!" Caney crowed, pleased to see her charge up and about.

Christy whisked into the room, took the chair next to Skye's, and jutted out her chin. "It's not as if I were Lazarus coming from the grave," she pointed out.

Caney took the sleeping baby carefully from Skye's arms and laid him in the nearby cradle, a sturdy pinewood piece that Trace had made as a gift, to go along with Bridget's blanket. "I'll just be gettin' myself into town," Caney said. "I done made up a basket lunch for me and Mr. Hicks to share."

Christy rolled her beautiful storm-cloud eyes, but a smile played at the corners of her mouth. "Miz Caney Blue, you are without shame. Why don't you just propose to the man and get it over with?"

Caney and Skye both laughed. Christy was beginning to sound like her old self.

" 'Cause I don't figure on scarin' him off," Caney answered a moment later. "You got to be careful, wooin' a man. Feed him and the like. Get him gentled down a bit, so he's fit to keep in the house."

Christy and Skye looked at each other, smiling.

"Good luck to you, then," Christy told their friend cheerfully. "I've been trying to 'gentle down' my Zachary since I met him. It's hopeless—he's as wild as ever." From the glow in her eyes, she didn't mind too much.

Caney gave Skye a pointed look. "Maybe I wasn't talkin' to you, Miss Christy," she said. "Maybe I was tryin' to plant an idea somewheres else." She waggled a finger for emphasis. "You want a man, you don't get him by chasin' him off your land and tryin' to hide your real feelin's, even from yourself. Men are skittish creatures, and a woman's got to handle 'em just so."

Skye averted her eyes. Were her feelings for Jake as painfully obvious as that?

Christy stepped in, bless her, before Skye was forced to answer. "You'll stop by the marshal's office, won't you? See if there's been any word from Zachary?"

Caney nodded. "I'll do that first thing," she said, and then she fetched her bonnet and cloak and left the house to start the long walk to town.

"Her heart's in the right place," Christy said, and patted Skye's hand reassuringly before pouring a cup of tea for herself.

"Does *everybody* know?" Skye burst out, chagrined.

Christy arched one dark, perfect eyebrow and raised the china cup to her lips. There was an unsettling twinkle in her eyes. "That you're smitten with Jake? Oh, yes, I suppose they do. Primrose Creek isn't exactly a den of secrets, is it?"

Skye's eyes went wide, and she knew she was blushing. "But how could—I wasn't even sure myself—"

Christy smiled. "Nevertheless, word's gotten out." An expression of sadness moved in her eyes. "Poor Jake. I had no business using him the way I did—"

"You never loved him at all?"

Christy shook her head. "No. I thought I could learn to, though. Thought that would be the best thing for Megan and for me, if I married Jake Vigil. Trouble is, I didn't consider what my plans might do to him." She looked away, looked back. "He's a good man, Skye. If you truly care for him, the way I care for Zachary and Bridget cares for Trace, then go after him. Personally, I think you and Jake would make a wonderful couple."

"Great Zeus," Skye murmured, for this was more than Christy had ever said about her brief engagement to Jake, at least to her. She set her own cup aside.

Christy was quiet for a long moment, rocking, sipping tea, gazing off into the ether. Then she looked at Skye again, and her expression was solemn. "You won't forget? To bring the Bible over, I mean?"

Skye was caught off-guard by something in her cousin's tone, even though she'd been the one to suggest that Christy and Zachary make an entry to record the birth of their first child. "Sure," she said.

Christy turned thoughtful again. "Thank you," she replied in a distracted tone of voice. Finally, she returned from her wanderings. "You haven't read the inscriptions lately, have you?" she asked. Their granddaddy had always called the list of births the McQuarry Begats, and the deaths and marriages had their monikers, too.

It was an odd question, even coming from Christy. She frowned. She hadn't seen the records since

Bridget had penned in Granddaddy's name as one of the departed, and that time her vision had been clouded by tears. "No. Christy, why?"

Like quicksilver, Christy changed the subject. "Has Jake declared himself?"

"Declared himself?" Skye scoffed, oddly relieved. Whatever Christy was alluding to concerning the entries in the family Bible, she wasn't sure she wanted to know it. "He thinks all the McQuarry women are trouble, plain and simple."

"You're trouble, all right, the whole bunch of you," put in a male voice from the direction of the doorway, "but I wouldn't call any of you plain, or simple, either."

"Zachary!" Christy cried in delight, standing so rapidly that she swayed and had to grasp the back of her chair for support.

Skye rose and steadied her by taking her elbow, watching as Zachary crossed the room toward his wife. He looked rumpled and unshaven, and devilishly handsome into the bargain. Drawing Christy up in his arms with a gentleness that made Skye's heart swell, he kissed her smartly. "I hear we have a son," he said, and his voice was gruff with emotion. "Sweetheart, I'm so sorry I wasn't here——"

By that time, Skye was almost to the threshold. She didn't bother to say good-bye, for Zachary and Christy Shaw were aware only of each other and the baby boy conceived of their passion.

Although she was happy for them, glad Zachary was back safe, there was a hollowness in her heart as she made her way down the slope and across the log bridge, headed for home.

Standing in the street, with the steam saws screaming in the mill behind him, Jake assessed the small boy standing before him with mingled amazement and rage. He was seven, he said, and the note pinned to his shabby coat confirmed that he was called Henry. The ordinary sounds of daily life in a bustling frontier town faded to a dull thrumming in Jake's ears as he regarded the child, unable—unwilling—to deny the reflection of his own features in that stubborn stance and small, upturned face. Grubby fists were clenched at the boy's sides, as if he expected to be sent away, and his hazel eyes snapped with obstinate dignity. Judging by the frail and spindly look of the lad, he'd gone a long while between meals more than just once or twice.

"Your mother sent you here?" It was a rhetorical question, really. The note, brief to the point of terseness, was signed in Amanda's hand. She'd been pregnant when she left Denver, and she'd never troubled herself to let Jake know. Now, tired of being "tied down," she was leaving the boy in his father's care.

Henry nodded his head. "Yes, sir. She did."

Jake folded his arms. "Where is she?"

"Last I seen her," Henry answered sturdily, though his voice trembled a little, "she was gettin' on a stage bound for San Francisco. Said there was a man there, goin' to marry her."

Jake closed his eyes. There weren't many women who would abandon their children, even in the worst of circumstances, but Amanda was about as motherly as a rabid she-weasel, and just as warmhearted. Typically, she'd chosen the worst possible time to take to her heels.

"If you don't want me," the boy said stalwartly, "I reckon I can make my own way."

Jake dropped to one knee and laid his hands gently on the small shoulders. "You're my son," he said, and had to clear his throat before he could go on. "Somehow, we'll work this through. In the meantime, you need something to eat and maybe a few hours of shut-eye."

The child looked so desperately relieved not to be turned away that Jake was forced to look to the side and blink a couple of times. Then he stood again. "Come along, then," he said in a hoarse voice. "Let's get you settled."

"That your place? Truly?" Henry asked a few minutes later, when they stood at the gate of Jake's grand and heretofore empty house. At Jake's nod, he gave a long, low whistle of exclamation through the gap between his front teeth.

They made their way to the kitchen, which was at the back of the house, and Henry gaped all the way. "This place is bigger'n anything I seen in Virginia City. Fancier, too. You got paintings of naked ladies?"

"That where you've been living? Virginia City?" Jake asked casually. He'd address the question of naked ladies later. Much later.

"Yup," the boy answered. "Mandy was servin' drinks there, at the Bucket of Blood."

Jake set his jaw. Serving drinks. He'd just bet. And how like Amanda to train her own child to call her by her first name. She'd probably told all her customers that Henry was her little brother and needed the poor kid's collaboration to keep up the pretense. "What about you? What did you do in Virginia City?"

"I went to school, some of the time leastways. Mostly, I just helped out at one of the livery stables. I didn't get a wage, exactly, but I had my meals with ole Squilly Bates, the blacksmith, and sometimes somebody would give me a nickel for groomin' a horse. I got a whole two bits once."

"So," Jake said, reaching the kitchen at last, pushing open the swinging door, "you're a workin' man. Where did you live?" He stepped into the pantry, came out with a wheel of cheese and a loaf of bread.

Henry's eyes widened at the sight of so much food, and he gulped visibly. Jake wasn't so sure, but he thought he'd heard the kid's stomach rumble. "I mostly just slept at the livery. In the hayloft. Mandy didn't really have no place to put me."

"I don't suppose she did," Jake murmured. When he'd met Amanda several years back in Denver, he'd mistaken her for an angel, and he'd fallen in love with her. She'd been raised like an alley cat, as it turned out, though she seemed determined to change, and Jake couldn't rightly fault a person for wanting to rise above a questionable past. After all, it wasn't her fault, her being born to a saloon girl, never knowing her father's name.

One fine day, though, she'd hauled off and shot

him in the shoulder with his own derringer, then cleaned out his private safe for good measure. Any sensible person would have thought she couldn't possibly stoop any lower than to try and kill the man she claimed to adore—but she had. Later, he'd learned that she had a husband tucked away somewhere, and she'd had some scuffles with the law, too.

Now, faced with his son, he knew that she'd robbed him of far more than the contents of his wallet and wall safe.

Damn her, she'd given birth to a child, unquestionably *his* child, and never told him the boy existed. He'd have taken the boy gladly, raised him as best he could, if only he'd known. Just then, if he could have gotten his hands on her throat—well, it didn't bear thinking about, what he might have done.

Belatedly, and with no little awkwardness, he pumped water and washed his hands at the iron sink, then set to slicing the bread and cheese. There was no milk, so he filled a glass with water from the pump. "Wash up over there at the sink, and have a chair," he said with a nod toward the table.

Henry obeyed and was soon seated, trying his best not to shove cheese and bread into his mouth with both hands. Jake felt a surge of sorrow for all the boy had done without, followed by a jolt of anger toward Amanda that was as sharp and pure as the thin air on a mountaintop.

He asked himself what in hell he was going to do now and was stuck for an answer. He couldn't let his business fold like a house of cards and walk away, not with a son to take care of. No, for Henry's sake and his own, he had to turn things around. Somehow.

He heard the echo of Malcolm's voice. *You could marry her.*

Marry Skye McQuarry? Not if his only other choice for a bride was a whore from Diamond Lil's. All the same, the idea of taking Skye to wife, and hence to his bed, sent an aching charge through his system to spark friction in every nerve ending he possessed. He imagined her soft skin, unveiled to him, imagined the scent of her hair . . .

Damnation. If he got down on bended knee, she wouldn't have him. And even if she agreed to a wedding, on some reckless impulse, she was sure to drive him insane from the time he said "I do" to the day after his funeral. No doubt, he'd have much the same effect on her.

He sighed.

"Are you sorry I came here?" Henry asked, his second hefty slice of buttered bread poised between his mouth and the tabletop. " 'Cause I can light out any time you say. Or maybe you have chores I could do to earn my keep—"

Jake crossed the room and ruffled the boy's hair with one hand. He was not a sentimental man, but in that moment, he very nearly scooped Henry up into his arms and embraced him. "Listen," he said quietly. "You'll have chores to do—every kid ought to help out—but you don't have to sing for your supper around here, understand? This is your home."

Henry looked bewildered. "It's a good thing I don't

have to sing," he said. "I sound 'bout like a frog when I try."

Jake laughed, and he realized it was the first time in many, many months. "You come by that honestly. I can't sing, either." He drew back a chair and sat down across from his son. *His son.* "You been using your mother's last name or mine?"

"I ain't required no last name, up to now," Henry replied. He'd reduced a large serving of yellow cheese to crumbs, and now he was looking at the remainder with an expression of longing. "Just Henry was all anybody needed to say. I knew they was talkin' to me."

Jake gave the boy more cheese. He'd have to lay in milk, and some eggs, too, among other things. Up to now, he'd taken most of his meals over at Diamond Lil's, but that would have to change. "I'd be real honored," he said, "if you'd call yourself Henry Vigil."

Henry blinked. "Really?"

Jake smiled, touched so deeply that it was a moment before he trusted himself to speak. "Really," he said.

Dawn had not yet spilled over the eastern mountains when Skye tumbled out of bed, got herself dressed in riding clothes, and headed for the barn, where she first fed all the animals, then saddled Bridget's mare, Sis. Riding astride, with a coil of rope secured to the saddle horn, she turned the little mare toward the high country, where she'd last seen the bay stallion. It was probably too much to hope that she would catch him, especially riding Sis, but she meant to try all the same.

The sun was full up by the time she found the stallion, and then it was his shrill cries of terror that drew her. She found him cornered in a canyon by a pack of wolves, and there she was, without a shotgun or even a derringer to scare the critters off with.

"Git!" she shouted to the wolves, and spurred Sis on with the heels of her boots. Sis was having none of it; she wheeled and tried to bolt in the other direction. Skye promptly brought her around again, keeping a short rein, lest the mare take the bit in her teeth and hightail it for the ranch.

Sis put up an argument and, with unaccustomed spirit, flung out both hind legs in a fairly respectable buck, landing in a spin. Skye sailed through the air and struck the ground with a bruising impact that stole her breath and made her see sparks of silver light. By the time she sat up, blinking the world back into view, and realized what a fix she'd gotten herself into, Sis was halfway home, and the wolves, all five of them, were taking more interest in her than in the stallion.

"Sweet Zeus," she swore, although she'd promised Bridget she'd break the habit of cussing, and she'd really tried, too. After gathering a rock in each hand, she scrabbled to her feet and faced her future, which did not look at all lengthy just then. Granddaddy's hat fell backward off her head, and her hair tumbled free of the few pins that held it. "You go on," she bluffed as the lead male, a scrawny, burr-covered beast with a grubby gray and white pelt, ambled toward her. "Git!"

The stallion had stopped carrying on and was awaiting his chance to make a run for it. The rest of the wolves, noting the leader's interest in this strange two-legged creature, had turned their massive heads, panting, to assess her.

Skye flung one of her precious rocks—they'd be on her before she could bend down to replace it with another—and took a stumbling step backward. "Help," she squeaked in a tiny voice, more because that was all she could think of than out of any expectation of rescue. "Somebody, *help*."

All the wolves were advancing toward her now, and, behind them, the bay stallion pawed the ground, ready to bolt for the hills but wisely biding his time, lest the pack give chase. With him would go all hope of capture, but Skye figured that didn't matter much anyhow, since she was about to be good and dead. She took another step back, and threw the second and last rock.

The crack of a rifle shot came in the next instant and startled her every bit as much as it did the wolves and the stallion. *That was some rock,* she thought for a portion of a moment, before the animals scattered and headed for the hills. Two more bursts of gunfire pursued them, for good measure. If the fellow firing that rifle was really trying to hit one of them, though, he was a poor shot, for the bullets pinged off the rocks and splintered a patch of bark off a tree, and that was all.

Skye whirled, one hand raised to shade her eyes, and saw Jake Vigil, of all people, mounted on his own impressive stallion. Without so much as a howdy-do, he went after the bay, rope in hand, and lassoed him in one throw.

Skye was livid, forgetting all about the wolf pack. She'd tracked that horse for months, and she wasn't about to let anyone take him from her, now or ever.

"That," she said when she was within shouting distance, "is *my* horse."

Jake was standing on the ground by then, holding his own against the stallion, still straining to break free and run. "I don't see your brand on him anywhere, Miss McQuarry. And by the way, you're welcome."

Skye's face went crimson, she could feel it, and her heart was beating hard enough to stampede right out of her chest. She told herself it was because of the wolves and because of the stallion, but she knew, deep down, that neither had much to do with her present distress. "What are you doing out here?" she demanded. "This is *my* land."

"This is Bridget's land," Jake corrected her calmly, keeping the lead rope taut as the stallion began to settle down a little. "As for what I was doing, that should be obvious. I was tracking this stallion. In point of fact, I've been after him since he was a yearling—I believe I told you that once."

Skye found her leather hat, plunked it on her head, and promptly hurled it to the ground again. Then she stomped on it with one foot, just for good measure, and Jake Vigil did the worst thing he possibly could have at that particular moment.

He threw back his handsome head and hooted with delight.

"Don't mention it," he said, as if she'd spoken, when at last he'd recovered himself, though there was laughter still lurking in his eyes. "Any time I can save your hide again, you just let me know."

Chapter

3

She'd made a perfect fool of herself, throwing her hat down like that, mashing the crown with one heel, but she didn't care. Damn Jake Vigil, anyhow, and damn whatever he thought of her as well, be it good or ill. She hadn't gone through all this, and nearly *died,* just so he could go merrily off with her horse.

"If you don't give me that animal right now, I'll have you arrested," she warned.

The stallion was frightened; no doubt, his nostrils were still full of the scent of wolf, and now he had a rope around his neck into the bargain. To him, one foe surely seemed as deadly as the other.

Jake worked deftly, gently, and spoke in a quiet voice as he calmed the poor beast. He didn't reply to Skye's challenge, which made her want to squash her hat into the dirt all over again.

"I can do it, too," she said. "My cousin is married to the marshal, you know."

He looked at her with an expression she couldn't read. He might have been seething, he might still have been laughing at her. Either one would be unacceptable. "Yes," he said evenly. "I know."

Skye regretted making such a silly statement and would have called it back if she could; surely, reminding Jake of the man Christy had married instead of him wouldn't help her case any. Besides, Zachary wasn't about to put a man in jail on her say-so, not for catching a wild horse before she did and refusing to hand it over, anyhow. In fact, she knew exactly what he'd say: *Possession is nine-tenths of the law.* Well, she darned well would have possessed that horse if it hadn't been for Jake Vigil's interference.

She bent down, snatched up her hat, and tried to salvage it by pushing at the inside of the crown with one fist. It was all she had left of her granddaddy, that old hat, and she felt almost as though she had desecrated something sacred by losing her temper the way she had.

"You ought to throw that thing away," Jake said in a tone of voice she'd never heard him use before. "The hat, I mean. It's not becoming—hides your hair."

His words gave Skye a sweet wrench; she prayed she wouldn't blush. He liked her hair? And what kind of silly thought was *that,* when the man was out-and-out stealing a stallion she'd had her eye on for weeks?

He ran a hand lightly down the length of the stallion's muzzle, but he was looking at Skye in an assessing way that made her deliciously uncomfortable and mad as a bee-stung grizzly with a toothache. "There is one way to settle our many differences, once and for all," he mused.

"I imagine there are several," Skye retorted. She tried to speak crisply, but her heart was skittering with anticipation and high dudgeon and profound relief that she hadn't tripped over her own tongue. Lord, but her emotions were so tangled, she didn't even hope to sort them out.

"A horse race," he said.

She stared at him. "A horse race?"

He grinned. "Yes. If you can beat me, riding this stallion," he said, indicating the bay, "he's all yours, and so is all the lumber you want for the house."

Skye could barely breathe. She hadn't lost a horse race since she was eight years old, and that time she'd been defeated by her father, one of the best riders in Virginia. "And if I lose?"

"Ah, if you lose," he said, pausing to ponder the prospect. It made him smile. "*If you lose,* Miss Mc-Quarry, you will marry me."

Her mouth dropped open, and she closed it with an effort. Her pulse thrummed in her ears, and the whole universe contracted to a space barely large enough to contain the two of them. She even felt dizzy. The nerve of the man. The very gall. She wanted to kiss him and kick him, both at once.

For some inexplicable reason, though, she didn't do either. He'd ambushed her tongue, and it only then broke free. "You—you want to m-marry me?" she blurted, and immediately longed for death. "Why?"

He drew closer, still holding the lead line with one

hand, and drew an index finger down the length of her nose. "Yes," he said. "I believe I do want to marry you, and I don't have the first idea why."

She was utterly confused. What was she doing, standing here letting him say such forward things? Why didn't she get a gun and shoot him? Why didn't she just say, straight out, that she would have married him anyway, right or wrong, win or lose, if he just asked her?

Because she was a McQuarry, that was why. She had more than the normal allotment of pride, even when that went against her best interests, but knowing this singular truth about herself didn't help overmuch. She was paralyzed, and her tongue felt thick in her mouth.

"Suppose I told you I've been lonely for a long time?" he asked quietly. Seriously. "That I'm tired of living by myself? Suppose I said I wanted a family?"

She folded her arms and waited. It was too good to be true, all of it. There had to be something more—and there was. Her trees. *He wants my timber.* She would have laid into him, if she'd been able to speak.

"Yesterday, a little boy turned up, quite literally on my doorstep," Jake said with a sigh. "Well, at the mill, anyway. Turns out, he's mine. His name is Henry, though I think Hank suits him better."

Skye recalled the boy she'd glimpsed the day before, perched in the box of a freight wagon, and found her voice at last. She had a deep affinity for children, especially little lost boys like Henry. "It 'turns out' he's yours? Didn't you know about him?"

Jake shook his head. "I wish I had. Things might have been different, for him and for me."

"You'd have stayed with his mother?"

"I didn't leave his mother," Jake said. "She left me. After shooting me in the shoulder with my own derringer and robbing me of every dime I had. I never saw her again."

"She sent the boy to you." Skye felt her brow crumple with confusion and concern. She was still bothered about the horse and the timber, but she'd pushed those concerns to the back of her mind for the moment.

Jake nodded. "From Virginia City."

She stared at him, confounded and oddly stung. It shouldn't have troubled her to hear that there had been other women in Jake's life, before Christy—of course there had—but it did. Oh, it did. "You were in love with a woman who shot you? What's *wrong* with you?"

He laughed, though there was a somber shadow in his eyes. "*She* shot *me*. I reckon the question ought to be 'What's wrong with her?' The answer is, 'One hell of a lot.' She's crazy, for one thing, and she's a liar, for another. Of course, she's a thief, too. But she's also beautiful and clever as all get-out, and she had me buffaloed, I guess. Until it was too late, anyhow."

Skye pushed her hair back from her face with a nervous gesture of one palm. "Damnation, I don't care about her."

"Then why did you ask?"

She wanted to fly at him; the trouble was, she didn't know what she'd do when she got there—claw his eyes right out of his head, or fling her arms around his neck and hold on for dear life. In the end, she decided to stay put.

"I didn't ask about her. I asked about you." She paused, drew a deep breath, and let it out again. "You want me to marry you because your son needs a mother."

"Something like that."

"Would I have my own room?"

"No," he said without hesitation. "I told you—I want a family, and that requires a real wife. I'm not interested in playing house."

Skye turned away, hoping she'd been quick enough to hide the color burning in her cheeks. "All this happens if I lose the horse race," she said, to clarify the matter a little. She still felt dazed. Just that morning, she'd gotten out of bed without a hope in Hades of marrying Jake Vigil, and now here he was, proposing to her. She would have been overjoyed, if it weren't for one thing—the union was merely a business arrangement to him; he hadn't mentioned love. He wanted her for the plainest and most practical of reasons, and he hadn't even bothered to pretend otherwise.

"Yes," he agreed, and when she looked again, her attention drawn by the familiar creak of leather, she saw that he'd mounted his horse, keeping the bay on a long lead. It wasn't a good idea to let two stallions get into close proximity; they tended to do battle, especially when the scent of wolf still lingered.

"When?" she asked, nearly choking on the word.

"Wh-when would we hold this race, I mean? And where?"

He smiled. "A week from Sunday ought to be soon enough. The road between Primrose Creek and my front gate should do as a course."

It was two miles from one point to the other, by Skye's estimation; not an unmanageable distance, certainly, for a pair of strong horses like these. But a week from Sunday! The bay wasn't even broken to ride yet, and besides, how was she going to train the animal to accept a rider if Jake insisted the stallion belonged to him? He obviously meant to take the bay back to town with him.

Jake made a gesture like tipping his hat, only he wasn't wearing one. Skye had long since noticed that he rarely did. "Deal?" he asked.

Skye gazed up at him. The sun was at his back, like an aura, putting her in mind of pagan gods—Apollo, perhaps, riding one of his chariot horses. She couldn't make out his features. "There's a lot we haven't settled," she pointed out.

He chuckled. "Now, that's a fact," he agreed. The leather of his saddle creaked again as he bent down, extending one hand and slipping his foot out of the stirrup so she could get a purchase to mount. "Come along, Miss McQuarry. I'll see you home, so the wolves don't get you."

She hesitated, then took his hand, planted her foot in the stirrup, and allowed him to pull her up behind him. Her precarious situation forced her to put both arms around his middle to keep from falling off, and the scents of his shirt and his skin and his hair combined to tug at her from the inside. The bay stallion trotted along behind them, as docile as could be.

"You'll have to leave that stallion here," she said when they'd reached Trace and Bridget's place and she'd gotten down from his horse, "if you expect me to make a saddle horse out of him in time for the race."

Jake looked back at the captured bay, as though assessing him. Then he leaned forward, resting one forearm across the pommel of his saddle. "That's just it, Miss McQuarry. I *don't* expect you to break him. You won't make much of a wife if you get yourself stepped on, thrown, or kicked."

"I've *been* stepped on, thrown, and kicked," she snapped, annoyed at his blithe assumption that she would lose their contest. At the same time, she was confused, because she *wanted* to marry him, which meant she'd have to lose. Didn't it? "I've been around horses all my life, *Mr.* Vigil, and I can't remember a time when I didn't ride."

"Riding is one thing," he pontificated from on high, "and saddle-breaking a wild horse is another. The question is decided."

Skye wanted to throw something. "If you think you can just announce that something is decided and go right on from there, whistling a tune—"

He grinned. "Are you backing out of our deal?"

She thought of all she stood to lose if she won that race and all she stood to gain if she lost. Pride wouldn't let her sacrifice the honor of winning, and love wouldn't let her claim it. She was in a dither, though she'd have gone back and found those wolves and fed herself to them before admitting as much.

"No," she answered at some length. "Are you?"

"Not a chance," he replied. "Hank and I, we need a woman in the house." Then he turned and rode cheerfully away toward town, leading the captured bay behind him.

"What was *that* all about?" a voice inquired, from just behind her.

Skye turned to see Megan standing there, holding one of Bridget and Trace's twins. And all of a sudden, Skye began to cry, to blubber and wail like a fool.

"Whatever is the matter?" Megan demanded, her eyes narrowed.

"I've just bet my whole future on a horse race!" Skye howled.

"Well, is that all?" Megan asked, a little impatiently. "What happens if you lose?"

Skye was stupefied by her cousin's blithe attitude, but she didn't bother to say so. It wouldn't have done any good. "I'll have to marry Jake Vigil."

Megan did not look the least bit sympathetic. "I see," she said, smirking a little. "I guess you're in some trouble, then. No McQuarry *I* ever heard of ever threw a race."

Skye was glum and, at one and the same time, possessed of a strange and secret jubilance. "Not one," she whispered miserably.

Megan's expression was tentative, almost wistful. Later, Skye would think she should have guessed, right then, what her cousin was planning to do. "We'll always be friends, won't we, Skye?" she asked. "Friends as well as cousins, no matter what?"

"Of course we will," Skye said. Her uneasiness deepened measurably and would not be ignored. "Megan, what are you—?"

"Skye!" Bridget interrupted from the doorway of the house. "Megan! Come inside, won't you? I need some help with the carding and spinning."

Skye and Megan looked at each other for a long, silent moment, and it was tacitly agreed that no more was to be said, at least in Bridget's presence.

Jake smiled to himself all the way to town, where he turned the bay stallion over to one of the stable hands at the livery for safekeeping. Leaning against the corral fence, he admired the animal for a while before deciding to head home.

The moment he took a step in that direction, however, he found himself face-to-face with Zachary Shaw. Once they had been good friends, but there had been a strain between them since the marshal had married Christy McQuarry.

Zach adjusted his hat. His stance and the set of his shoulders gave clear indication that he had something to say and meant to say it, no matter how unwelcome the observation might be. "That's a fine animal," he said.

"Thanks," Jake replied without inflection. "No matter what your wife's sister might have told you, I caught that stallion myself, and I mean to put my brand on him, if matters come to that."

The marshal frowned, plainly puzzled. So, Jake

thought, Skye hadn't run to her cousin's husband, the marshal, to stake a claim of her own to the bay. She went up another notch in his estimation. "What the hell are you talking about?"

Jake nearly laughed. Nearly but not quite. "Never mind that. If you have business with me, let's hear it. Otherwise, I'll be making my way back to the mill."

Shaw sighed. They were standing on Primrose Creek's only real street, two men known to have their differences. Boggle-eyed passers-by were stretching their ears in the effort to eavesdrop. "Damn it, Jake, listen to me. There are a couple of agents over at Diamond Lil's, making a lot of noise about taking over your whole operation by the end of the month. I thought you might want to know."

Jake tightened his jawline, and the joint made a faint popping sound when he released it by force of will. He glanced in the direction of the saloon, which was only one of several that had sprung up in Primrose Creek over the past few years and subsequently prospered. "Thanks," he said in a virtual growl.

"Is it true, Jake?" Zachary asked quietly. "Are you in trouble?"

There was no reason to tell his erstwhile friend about the deal he'd made with the railroad and all he stood to lose if he didn't keep up his end of the bargain. It was literally everything he could do not to storm down the street to Diamond Lil's and bang a few heads together. At last, he met the other man's gaze squarely. "No need for you to be concerned," he said coolly. "It's nothing I can't handle."

Shaw sighed. "Are you going to hold that grudge of yours until some undertaker pulls off your boots once and for all, or what?"

Jake stiffened; automatically, his right hand clenched into a fist, then relaxed again. "Malcolm tells me you're a father," he said, ignoring the question. "Congratulations." With that, he walked away, moving in the general direction of Diamond Lil's, even though it was against his better judgment.

But Shaw wasn't through with him yet. "Jake."

He stopped, refusing to turn around again, and waited.

"I didn't tell you about those railroad agents so you could head down there and tear the saloon apart. Whoever makes trouble, whether it's them or you, will end up in my jail for the night, if not longer. Clear?"

Jake didn't offer a verbal reply, but his opinion must have been obvious anyway in the sudden stiffening of his spine and the length of his strides. He reached the entrance of the saloon and was just about to push through the swinging doors and step over the threshold when Hank appeared at his side, seemingly out of nowhere.

"Pa?" he asked. The kid was still getting used to having a father—hell, Jake was just getting used to *being* one—and the word came out like a croak.

Jake closed his eyes for a moment. *Not now,* he thought. Then he looked down at his son. "Aren't you supposed to be in school?" he asked. He'd extracted a solemn promise from Hank, early that same morning, that he'd avail himself of Primrose Creek's makeshift schoolhouse.

"I ain't goin' back to that place ever," Hank announced. "There's nobody there but for a pack of runny-nosed kids and that homely teacher."

Jake, mad enough to bite through a railroad spike an instant before, now had trouble holding back a grin. At the edge of his vision, he glimpsed Zachary Shaw, pretending to look at a display of feathered hats and other female fripperies in the milliner's window. Miss Ingmire, the schoolmarm, was only seventeen herself, according to rumor, and she had trouble keeping order in class. As for the runny-nosed kids, well, Jake figured there was probably room for one more; his boy would fit right in.

He stepped aside, one hand resting on Hank's blade-thin little shoulder. "I'm afraid there are some things in this life that we don't have a choice about, and school is one of them. You'll need to read and write and cipher if you're going to run my timber company someday." Provided there still *was* a company once Hank was grown. The way things were going, they'd both end up as drifters and no-accounts.

Unless, of course, he won next Sunday's horse race—as he fully intended to do. Surely, he'd be able to persuade Skye to let him harvest the necessary timber once they were man and wife. He would run double and even triple shifts at the mill and meet the railroad's deadline. His spirits rose, and he grinned. "Suppose I told you that you were about to get yourself a mother. What do you think she'd have to say about a boy who won't go to school?"

Hank's square little chin jutted out a little, and his

eyes snapped. "If she's anything like Mandy, I'll be taking to the road again, and it won't matter *what* she thinks. I ain't puttin' up with no ear-washing, neither."

Jake bit the inside of his cheek in order to maintain the sober expression he'd just managed to assume. "She's nothing like Amanda," he assured the boy. "I think you'll like her."

Hank narrowed his eyes. "She'll want me to go to school every day, though. Maybe even church on Sundays."

" 'Fraid so," Jake admitted. "Women place a lot of store by school and churchgoing. I believe the Reverend Taylor likes to cut loose with an extra sermon on Wednesday nights, too."

Hank sighed, and his shoulders slumped significantly, though Jake thought he sensed a certain excitement in the child. No doubt, he'd dreamed of being an ordinary kid many a time, with an ordinary father and mother and a set of rules to follow.

"Let's go on home," Jake said quietly. "You can make another try at school tomorrow."

Hank hesitated, then fell into step beside him.

A voice from behind stopped both of them cold. "Vigil!"

Jake turned. Two strangers stood on the wooden walkway outside Diamond Lil's, and he knew by their waistcoats and derby hats that they were railroad men. His hand came to rest lightly on top of Hank's head. "I don't conduct my business in the streets, gentlemen," he said. "You have something to say to me, you come to my office at the mill in the morning."

The taller of the two men, a thin, pockmarked fellow with overlapping front teeth, worked up a smile. "No offense meant," he said, and touched the brim of his hat in a gesture that conveyed more mockery than respect. "We'll be around to see you first thing."

"I reckon you know what it's about," put in the second agent. He was little and wiry, the kind a man had to look out for in a fight.

Jake didn't reply. He simply turned his back on the two men and started toward home again. Zachary, who evidently had stuck to Jake's heel like a chunk of horse manure, fell into step beside him. After a friendly nod of acknowledgment to the boy, he got right down to business. "It's time we put what happened behind us, Jake. Time like this, a man needs his friends."

Jake glared at him and kept walking. "I'll remember that," he said, "if I run into any."

Shaw looked downright exasperated. "Damn it," he rasped. Then, remembering Hank, he lowered his voice, as if that would keep a sharp-eared kid from hearing. *"Damn it,"* he repeated. "I'm trying to help you here!"

Jake gave a derisive chuckle. "Five minutes ago," he said, "you were threatening to throw me in jail."

"I still might," the marshal said lightly. "Even if there isn't a law against your kind of pig-headed, jackass approach to life, there ought to be. Now, I have another question. Two, in fact. Where did you get this kid? And did I hear him call you Pa?"

* * *

When a brisk knock sounded at his office door the next morning, an hour after he'd coerced Hank into returning to school and its many trials and crossed the street to the mill, Jake sighed with resignation. Sooner or later, he'd have to speak with the railroad people, anyway. It might as well be sooner.

"Come in," he growled.

He couldn't have been more surprised when Skye McQuarry answered his summons, clad in a yellow dress with ruffles at the cuffs and hemline. Her rich brown hair was pinned up in a loose knot at the back of her head, and her skin and eyes glowed, even as a nervous blush rose in her cheeks.

He stood so hastily that he nearly overturned his chair, and for a long moment, he just stared at her like a smitten boy, too startled to speak. She'd been pretty before, in her rough clothes and that old leather hat with the floppy brim, but she was beautiful now.

Something in his discomfiture must have given her confidence, for she straightened her shoulders and met his gaze straight on. "We need to clarify a few matters," she said. "If I lose this race—which I won't—and have to marry you, will you promise to treat me with respect? I won't put up with anything less. I expect to be a partner to you, and I will not be made to do anything I don't choose to do."

Jake Vigil found his tongue. "Yes," he said. Then he cleared his throat, still profoundly stricken by the sight and scent of her, by his sudden and fierce desire to reach out and pull her into his arms, and said it again. "Yes, Skye. I promise." He paused. "God knows, I have my faults, but I'm not the kind to take advantage of a woman." While the words he spoke were truthful, he had to admit he wasn't following her train of thought that well, stunned as he was by her unexpected appearance.

She looked as though she believed him. Could it be that she actually *wanted* this marriage? No, it couldn't be that.

"Thank you," she said, and turned to go.

"Skye?" He couldn't help himself; her name was out of his mouth like a cat slipping through an open doorway.

She faced him again and raised one eyebrow, waiting for him to speak.

"You'll want to be sure and win that race if you can," he heard himself tell her. "Just now, my prospects as a husband and provider are not exactly impressive."

She smiled again, and again he was thunderstruck. Had Christy's smile ever affected him like that? Had Amanda's? He couldn't remember feeling this way—pleasantly off-balance—in the whole of his life.

"Don't worry," she said. "Mine are excellent."

"Your—?" He was furiously embarrassed and not sure why.

"Prospects," she explained, and let herself out.

He was still standing up, still staring at the empty doorway, when the two railroad agents appeared, hats artfully in hand, manners humble.

"Sit down," he said, and tried to remember why they were there.

"About your contract with the Union Pacific," began the tall one, dragging a chair up in front of Jake's desk while his partner did the same. "There seems to be some concern among the board of directors—"

Jake sank into his own chair and shoved a hand through his hair. "Gentlemen, I gave my word that I will deliver thirty thousand railroad ties within the next few weeks, and I mean to keep it." *How?* he asked himself. Even if Skye granted him access to her precious trees, he'd have trouble meeting the deadline, which was just a month away.

"How?" asked the second agent, crossing his legs at the knee.

"Is the order overdue?" Jake countered.

The agents reddened, and one of them curled a finger beneath his collar and tugged. "Not exactly."

That was when Jake faced the truth: the railroad was going to win either way. If they couldn't get the railroad ties, they'd have his holdings—the mountain he had fought and worked to own, the house he'd built, the equipment, and the thriving mill. Hell, maybe they'd have the whole damn town by the time they got through.

He sat back in his chair and interlaced his fingers, primarily to keep himself from springing over the desk and throttling the both of them, one gullet in each hand.

"According to our contract," said one agent, uncomfortable in the thunderous silence, "you still have thirty days. But you don't seem to be making much progress, and it would be impossible, in such a short time—"

Jake thought of Skye and of Hank. Not so long ago, he'd almost been discouraged enough to give up, count himself a fool for staking everything he had on this one deal, and move on. Now, it seemed to him, he had every reason to fight, every reason to succeed.

"You'll have your timber if I have to sell my soul to get it," he said. "Now, get out. I have work to do."

Skye went by the livery stable, after she left Jake, to look in on the bay. Sure enough, two of the hands were hard at work, trying to break him to ride, and they weren't having much luck.

She leaned against the fence, unmindful of her good dress, her dainty slippers, her carefully coiffed hair. She was so used to wearing boots, homespun skirts and blouses, and Granddaddy's hat that she forgot to fuss.

The stallion was a magnificent sight, his muscles clearly defined and powerful, his spirit so strong that Skye felt akin to him. Oh, yes, they were going to win the race on Sunday, she and the bay.

Zachary came to stand beside her at the fence, his folded arms resting on the top rail, his grin warm and full of amusement. "Well, now, who's this? Though you bear a strong resemblance to somebody I know, I don't think I recognize you."

Skye laughed. "Was that a compliment or an insult?" she asked.

"Most definitely a compliment," he replied, and his

grin broadened. "Isn't this the horse you've been tracking for the last six months?"

She'd tried to keep her plans a secret, confiding only in Megan, but it was obvious that her cousin had told Christy, and Christy had told Zachary. All inclination to smile gone, she bit her lower lip before answering. "That's him," she said. "Jake Vigil got to him before I did."

"Hmmm," Zachary mused. "Almost seems like he knew you wanted that horse and got the drop on you deliberately, doesn't it? I guess he figured the bay would make a strong drawing card."

Skye felt the pit of her stomach slip. "Why should he want a drawing card?" she asked, even though she already knew. God help her, she knew.

Zachary sighed. "I guess he figures he might be able to swap you that horse for the rights to your timber," he said.

All Skye's pretty, fragile dreams collapsed in the space of a moment. She'd been deluding herself, and on purpose, too. Once she was Jake's wife, he could cut down the tallest and best trees and saw them up into railroad ties if he wanted. He'd probably lose interest in her once he'd gotten his way—he might even find an excuse to secure a divorce, though it was more likely he'd simply go right on taking his pleasure with the hurdy-gurdy women, the way other men did.

She had almost made a terrible mistake. She would not be able to endure the outrage, the humiliation of such an arrangement, not even for love.

As for Jake, well, he was *that* sure he would win the race, the arrogant scoundrel.

"Skye?" Zachary looked concerned.

"We'll just see," she sputtered, taking a handful of skirt on either side.

Zachary's worried expression changed to one of bafflement. "See what?" he asked.

But Skye was already spinning away on one heel, bent on going back to Jake Vigil's office, giving him a piece of her mind, and telling him that his devious plan had failed. The bet was off.

He didn't need to know that he had broken her heart.

Zachary reached out and caught hold of her arm, pulling her around to face him again. "Whoa," he said. He and Trace were both protective of her and Megan, as well as their wives. Much as she loved them, she often found them irritating. Did they think she was a child, helpless and without guile? "You look like you're about to shoot somebody."

Tears burned in her eyes; humiliated, she tried to blink them away.

That was enough for Zachary. He tugged her right across the street to his office. Once they were inside, he sat her down in a chair, hung his hat on a peg by the door, and poured two cups of his infamously bad coffee. He set one down in front of her on the surface of his desk and grinned. "Tell me what's the matter," he teased, "or I'll make you drink it."

Skye sniffled. "I want to report a horse theft," she said.

"What?"

"That horse was mine. I tracked it for months. I want Jake Vigil arrested for robbery."

Zachary rounded his desk and sat down heavily in his chair. "Well, now," he said reflectively, putting his feet up to rest on top of a stack of wanted posters. "This situation is getting more interesting all the time."

"You have to do something."

Zachary sighed. "Skye, I can't arrest a man without cause, and you know it. Now, I want you to calm down and promise me you won't do anything stupid."

Skye couldn't make such a promise, and it was a damn good thing she didn't. It would have been impossible to keep.

Chapter

4

❦

The livery stable was dark, and the bay stallion wasn't in the corral.

Skye, clad for skulking in trousers, one of Trace's hats, and a dark coat, dragged a bale of hay over to a window and climbed onto it to peer inside. She had no real experience as a horse thief, since the worst thing she'd ever done was borrow her daddy's favorite gelding without asking. She'd been thrown and gotten a broken arm for her trouble, along with a blistering lecture from her furious grandfather, delivered when she'd had some time to mend and to reflect upon the error of her ways.

As her eyes adjusted to the gloom, she spotted the bay in a nearby stall. Someone had put a feedbag on him, and, in that innocent stance, he looked as if he might have spent the day pulling a buggy or trotting smartly through a big-city park with a well-dressed rider on his back.

She blew out a sigh and reminded herself that she had every right to ride the bay if she wanted; he was really hers, after all. She had been the one to track the critter, and in her heart she had laid claim to him long before Jake Vigil came along and all but grabbed him out from under her. Of course, the law—namely Zachary—definitely would not see the matter the same way.

She'd brought along her own bridle, and she tossed it through the window first, to keep herself from turning coward at the last second. Then she climbed over the sill, one leg at a time, and jumped to the straw-covered floor, hardly making a sound in the process. Although several of the horses snuffled and whinnied, she didn't hear what she had dreaded most: a human voice issuing a challenge to a trespasser. She stood very still for a few moments nonetheless, waiting for her heart to slide down out of her throat and the blood-thunder to subside from her ears. She stooped to pick up the bridle. Then, moving slowly, murmuring nonsensically in what she hoped was a reassuring tone, she approached the bay.

The animal snorted and shifted nervously between the high rails of his stall, and Skye held her breath. Orville Hayes, the old reprobate who lived in a back room and kept watch over the stock at night to earn his keep, was busy swilling spirits at the Golden Garter, as usual. Skye had paused outside the saloon on her way to the livery and dared to look over the swinging doors, just to make sure. Mr. Hayes had been at the bar, all right, bending his elbow and thereby neglecting his duties at the stable.

"Easy," she whispered to the horse. "Take it easy."

Miraculously, the stallion settled down a little.

Skye had no idea whether or not anyone had managed to ride him since his capture the morning before, but it didn't seem likely. It took days, sometimes weeks, to break a horse to the saddle, and occasionally the task proved downright impossible. If she was going to ride the stallion in Sunday's race, he had to be green-broke, at least.

"Easy," she said again. The stall gate squealed a little as she opened it. She stepped inside, one hand resting lightly on the stallion's flank in an effort to keep him from panicking, and moved alongside, trailing her fingertips over his gleaming hide until she was within his range of sight.

She patted the bay's forehead and gave him a lump of sugar from the flat of her palm, careful to keep her fingers out of the way.

When she dared, she slowly raised the far side of the earpiece into place. He sputtered a protest but didn't commence to kicking and carrying on—if he had, she'd probably have been trampled to something with the consistency of cornmeal mush—and Skye was heartened. She eased the leather strap over the other ear and balanced the bit on her open palm.

"You need a name," she said as the stallion took the questionable offering. She slid the metal bar carefully back over his tongue until it rested behind his teeth and finished buckling the bridle into place with swift motions of her hands, so long practiced as to be second nature. "How about Lancelot? Do you like that?"

The bay nickered and pranced a little, but he allowed her to guide him backward, out of the stall. It was too bad horse-thieving was a crime, Skye thought, for she certainly seemed to have the knack.

Outside, in the moonlight and the glow of saloon lamps, Skye stood, reins in hand, and spoke to the horse again in an earnest whisper. "Now, you listen here. I have to win this race on Sunday afternoon, and to do that, I need your help. I'll thank you to cooperate because, if you don't, I'm going to be a disgrace to every McQuarry who ever drew breath." She bit her lip and blinked back tears.

She could spare the timber Jake wanted, as long as it was cut responsibly, Trace and Zachary had convinced her of that, albeit with some difficulty. But now, faced with the reality, the mere thought of a lifetime passed with a husband who didn't love her was intolerable. She'd seen real love up close, between Bridget and Trace and between Christy and Zachary, the kind that flowed both ways. She wanted the same sweet secrets, the same private laughter, the same fierce passion and partnership of souls.

"All right," she said, as much to herself as to the stallion, who was still nameless since he hadn't shown any particular fondness for Lancelot. "We're in this together, you and me, and if we're going to win, we have to trust each other." With that, she closed her eyes, sent a silent but fervent prayer winging to heaven, and sprang onto the bay's back.

He stood still as death for what seemed a long while, every muscle bunched, as if about to fly apart in pieces like a clay pot left too long on the fire. Then he quivered slightly through the belly and flanks and snorted a clear warning. The next few instants would tell it all: he might buck like the devil, or he might let her ride. She knew not which, and she wasn't sure he did, either.

Her throat was dry, and her heart pounded. Gently, she patted the animal's corded, sweating neck. "Easy," she said, and that, too, was second nature, the word her granddaddy had always used with nervous horses. "Take it real easy. I'm not going to hurt you, and I'd appreciate the same favor in return, if you can see your way clear not to throw me."

The bay was clearly the kind to deliberate, and he must have debated the question from both sides and in considerable depth, for they sat like a war monument, the two of them, for what seemed the best part of a month. While Skye waited, she tried not to imagine herself hurtling through the night air or rolling on the ground in a vain attempt to avoid four hard hooves. When he didn't rear, Skye was pleasantly surprised, and while she was congratulating herself on her way with horses, he bolted. By the time they reached the edge of town, he seemed bent on sprouting wings, like Pegasus, and taking to the air. It didn't occur to Skye to draw back on the reins and slow him down; instead, she tightened her legs around the barrel of his body and crouched low over his neck, brimming with joy.

"He's gone," Orville Hayes whined, twisting his hat in his hands as he stood blinking his rheumy eyes in the dazzling sunlight outside Jake's office. "Mr. Vigil, that fine stallion of yours is just plain *gone*. Somebody stolt him."

Jake resisted an urge to grasp the old man by the lapels and wrench him onto the balls of his feet. *"What?"* he demanded, even though he'd heard Orville's words all too clearly. "Where the devil were *you* when this happened?"

Orville swallowed visibly and crumpled the hat still further in his nervousness. "I stepped down to the Golden Garter—just long enough to have a single drink, mind you—Lil done cut off my credit a long time ago—and when I got back—"

Jake glanced pointedly in the direction of the sun, which was well above the eastern horizon. "When you got back, you were so drunk that the stables could have burned down around your ears without your knowing," he finished, disgusted but resigned. "When, exactly, did you discover that my horse had been stolen?"

"J-just a little while ago," Orville confessed. "You ain't gonna get me into no dutch with Lil, are you, Mr. Vigil? I lose this job, I don't know what I'm gonna do—"

Jake sighed, resting his hands on his hips, and considered the situation. Orville worked for none other than the illustrious Diamond Lil; besides running a thriving saloon and brothel, the lady owned the stables and several other businesses in town, and she was hardheaded. Turning her loose on poor old Orville wouldn't get the stallion back, and besides, Jake had a pretty good idea who the culprit was, anyhow. If he found Skye McQuarry, chances were good that he'd find the bay, too.

He rubbed his chin. "I don't know," he said in a noncommittal tone of voice. "Fact is, if you worked for me, I'd show you the road."

Orville did not dare to point out that he didn't work for Jake; it would have been worse than stupid, given the circumstances. "I came and tolt you right away, didn't I?" he half whined, his countenance having slipped from fawning to outright pitiful. "I ain't even been over to tell the marshal yet."

"I'll take care of that," Jake said tightly. He didn't plan to speak to Zachary just yet himself. No, it was someone else he wanted to see. He felt a strange, elemental stir deep within him, just anticipating the coming encounter with Skye McQuarry. "You go on about your business, and I'll see to the horse thief."

"You know who done it?" Among Orville's other unredeeming qualities were a nosy nature and a tendency to gossip like an empty-headed spinster.

Jake ignored the question. "Get my horse saddled," he said, speaking of Trojan, the stallion he'd owned for the last several years. Then he turned to head for the mill, where he told his foreman he'd be gone awhile. Hank was over at the schoolhouse, and it looked as if the boy was finally going to stay put, so he could concentrate on catching up with Miss McQuarry. It shouldn't be difficult.

Ten minutes later, he was riding out of town, half amused and half furious. On the one hand, he had to admire Skye's audacity, not to mention her riding skills. On the other, he wanted to yell at her until his voice rang off the mountainsides. Damn fool woman. Didn't she know a wild horse was dangerous—especially a stallion? By now, she might well have gotten herself stomped to death or broken that stiff McQuarry neck of hers.

A rush of cold horror coursed through his system. Maybe she *had* been hurt or killed. Maybe she was already lying on the ground someplace, dead or dying. In pain.

He gave the horse his heels and reached Trace and Bridget's place in a matter of minutes. Bridget met him in the dooryard, shading her eyes from the bright sunlight with one hand. Her smile might have warmed him if he hadn't been so wrought up over Skye and the stallion.

"Jake! What brings you here? I'm afraid Trace is away from home, taking a string of saddle horses down to Fort Grant."

"I'm not looking for Trace," Jake said. He was trying to be polite, but his words came out sounding terse. "Is your sister around?"

She frowned. "I suppose Skye's around here somewhere—she'd already left the house when I got up this morning. She's probably upstream panning for gold or traipsing around someplace in those woods of hers." Bridget paused, probably regretting that she'd mentioned the timber, a known bone of contention between Jake and Skye. "Is—is something wrong?"

Jake managed to smile, though he suspected it

looked as forced as it felt, just wobbling there on his face, like a bill held to a brick wall with nothing but spit. "She borrowed something of mine," he said in what he hoped was a jovial tone. "I'd like to get it back."

Bridget sighed. "Well, when you see her, you tell her to get on home, please. I need some help setting out onion starts, and it's wash day, too."

He nodded, thought briefly, and then, on a hunch, started toward the high meadow just below the timberline, where he'd caught the bay only the morning before. Had it really been just a day since then? He felt as though he'd lived a lifetime in the interim, and he expected to battle his way through ten more before dinnertime.

She was there with the stallion, and when Jake caught sight of her, he drew up on his reins and sat back in the saddle, watching her. He was spellbound, a wanderer come upon a graceful nymph, unable to speak or move for the awe of it. His breath caught in his throat and lodged there like a peach pit. He felt a wild mingling of gratitude and fury, terror and pure, primitive joy.

As he looked on, Skye rode fluidly, proudly, guiding the stallion in a wide circle through the high, sweet grass. She'd left the hat at home, evidently, or lost it someplace, for her dark brown hair flowed behind her in the breeze, as rich and wild and shining as the bay's wind-ruffled mane.

When she caught sight of him, she did not even break stride, though she did rein the stallion in his direction. Her smile was saucy as she faced him, easing the splendid horse to a stop and leaning down to pat his neck.

"I thought as much," he ground out. He was so stricken, all of a sudden, that he couldn't manage anything more.

There was an impish light in her wide brown eyes. She murmured something unintelligible and fond to the stallion, and for the first time in his life, Jake Vigil found himself envying a horse. "He needed to get used to me," she explained, sitting easy in the saddle while the bay danced, eager to run again, "and I needed to get used to him. I'm sure we can win the race, he and I, now that we're friends."

"How do you know I'm not going to have you jailed for thieving before Sunday?" he demanded. He'd had some trouble finding his voice, and when he did, it came out loud as thunder.

She didn't so much as flinch at the prospect of spending time behind bars. Of course, she wouldn't. Zachary Shaw, the marshal, was a member of the family, and even if he *wanted* to arrest her, he'd catch hell at home if he did. "I don't think you'd do that," she said easily.

"Just remember our terms," Jake snapped. "When I win, you'll marry me. No heel dragging, no questions asked."

Something unreadable flickered in her eyes and was gone. "I remember," she said almost sadly. Then she perked up again. "Since *I* intend to come in first, though, I'm not the least bit worried."

Jake remained firmly convinced of his own proficiency when it came to horses, but here he was, having to *coerce* a woman into becoming his bride, and that didn't set well. In fact, it was downright galling. Even facing financial ruin, he was a better catch than most of the men in town—he was strong and smart, clean and fairly presentable into the bargain, and if all his plans went to hell and he lost everything he had, he knew he could build another fortune, in another place, just by pushing up his sleeves, spitting on his hands, and getting to work. He'd be a good father to his newfound son, and to any subsequent children, and a fine mate as well . . .

Just briefly, tossing in the wake of these thoughts, he considered proposing to Skye McQuarry right then and there, just asking her to forget the race and marry him, but all of a sudden, his collar tightened like a noose, cutting off his air, and the pit of his stomach clenched painfully. Women wanted "I love you's" and promises and all sorts of pretty words, and he was no poet—he'd gone numb inside when he lost Christy. No, it had happened even before that, he realized. Something had withered within him when he saw Amanda for who she truly was, and he'd only kidded himself into believing he loved Christy.

"Mr. Vigil?" Skye prompted, brow slightly furrowed.

He realized that he'd left the conversation hanging at some length. She'd said something cocky with regard to their upcoming contest, and furthermore, she looked disappointed that he hadn't responded in kind. "I was just imagining our wedding night," he said, though he hadn't been. Until then, that is. Now his mind was full of Skye—the scent and softness of her hair, the sound of her voice, urging and then pleading and finally sighing, the limber and luminous contours of her body, bared to him in trusting abandon.

She reddened right up, and her mouth tightened for a moment, and Jake felt jubilation, in addition to the inevitable discomfort such ideas caused.

"Why wait until Sunday?" she demanded, eyes flashing. "Why don't we settle this right now? First one to town wins."

Jake considered the suggestion, and one word thrummed through his spirit, soul, and body, powerful as a tremor in the ground. *Tonight.*

"All right," he said, amazed that the sound came out whole. He fairly choked on that simple phrase, realizing, as he did, how very much hung in the balance. "Count of three?"

She aligned the stallion alongside his with such skill that for the length of a heartbeat, he actually considered that she might reach the edge of Primrose Creek proper before he did. "Count of three," she agreed.

"One," Jake said, bracing himself.

"Two," Skye continued.

"Three!" Jake yelled, and took his stallion from a standstill to a gallop in one short leap.

Skye kept up with him, leaning low over the bay's neck, and once or twice Jake nearly unseated himself for looking at her instead of the trail ahead. God in heaven, but she was a beautiful sight, as at home on that wild horse as if she were part of him.

They rushed between copses of trees, birch and

aspen but mostly pine, slapped and clawed by low-hanging branches, and came across the Qualtroughs' land, splashing through the dazzle-bright creek, neck-and-neck. Out of the corner of one eye, Jake caught a glimpse of Bridget and Megan, Christy's pretty redheaded sister, beaming and clapping their hands together. Plainly, Skye had confided in them about the wager, but there was just no telling whom they were rooting for, Jake thought distractedly. They were an odd bunch, those McQuarrys.

A two-mile stretch lay ahead, once they'd crossed the water; it was rutted and narrow in places, with steep dropoffs and sharp turns, and Jake was torn. On the one hand, he wanted to win, wanted it more than he'd ever wanted anything before, but he was aware of Skye's growing recklessness, too, and he was afraid for her. When it came to horses, the woman apparently didn't have a sensible bone in her body; she rode full-out, hell-bent-for-election, with an absence of fear that astounded him.

The town came into view, and they thundered toward it, the hooves of the two stallions pounding drumlike on the hard, dry ground. Jake waited until the last possible moment, then spurred his mount into a final burst of speed, and Skye did the same. He crossed the agreed-upon finish line a half-length ahead of her and wheeled the stallion around just in time to see the bay miss a step and send his rider soaring over his head before catching himself.

Jake watched in horror as Skye rolled end-over-end in midair, a process that seemed to take an unaccountably long time, given that no more than a few moments could have passed. Long before he'd jumped from the saddle and run toward her, she landed flat on her back, arms outspread, with a wallop that reverberated through Jake's own system.

He knelt beside her, frantic, the stallions forgotten behind him. "Skye!" he called, afraid to touch her and yet barely able to resist the urge to gather her close and hold her against his chest. It wouldn't do to move her if anything were broken, and given the spill she'd taken, that seemed pretty likely. "Are you hurt?"

She blinked up at the blue sky, as though trying to remember where she'd seen it before, and then began to breathe again, slowly and carefully. "I don't—th-think so," she said. "Just let me lie here a second—till I get my wind back." She took a few shaky breaths. "I've got to stop doing this."

He smoothed her hair away from her forehead. There were smudges of dirt on her cheeks, but somehow that only made her prettier. "I'll help you up when you're ready," he said stupidly. He had to say *something*, after all, and nothing else came to mind.

She drew in a deep breath, let it out, drew in another. Jake watched, captivated, as her shapely breasts rose and fell with the motion, then realized what a liberty he'd taken and blushed.

She sighed, though he would have sworn he saw laughter playing hide-and-seek in her eyes, and started to sit up on her own. "I guess you win," she said with a sort of breezy resignation.

Jake sat back on his heels. He'd *won*. Damn if he

hadn't forgotten all about the race for worrying about the prize. "I guess so," he said, bemused.

She was scrambling to her feet, and Jake, profoundly disconcerted, scrambled with her. He wasn't sure he'd been of any help, though, when they stood facing each other there in the dust. Her lower lip trembled, but there was a proud set to her chin.

"You don't have to do this," he heard himself say. Where the hell had *that* come from? Timber and horse be damned—if he couldn't bed this woman, and soon, he was going to calcify.

Her chin rose another notch, and her expression was solemn. She dusted off her trousers without looking away from his face. "A deal," she said, "is a deal."

Jake was at once exultant and scared out of his long-johns. "Right." He ground out the word. "A deal is a deal."

She flushed prettily, and he saw her throat move as she swallowed. "I'd—I'd like to go home first. Talk to my family—wash up a little—put on a dress—"

"I'll speak to Judge Ryan," he said. "Reverend Taylor's gone to Denver to visit his daughter."

She nodded, gathered the bay's reins into one hand, and climbed into the saddle with an ease Jake couldn't help admiring. She had courage aplenty, that was for sure, getting back on a horse right after a nasty tumble. "I imagine my sister and cousins will want to be there. Caney, too, of course."

"Two o'clock?" he said, lightheaded and a little dazed, without even a hard fall from the saddle for an excuse.

"Two o'clock," she confirmed, and he thought he saw just the faintest hint of a smile flash in her eyes before she reined the bay around and started back toward the creek.

"You lost that race on purpose!" Megan accused in a delighted whisper as she fastened the row of small buttons at the back of Skye's best dress, a pale peach organza with lace at the collar and cuffs. She'd sent away for the frock, all the way to Chicago, Illinois, with some of her first earnings from the gold-panning enterprise.

Skye assessed her image in the looking glass affixed to the wall of Bridget and Trace's bedroom, holding a fold of skirt in either hand and whirling slowly, once to one side and once to the other. She was a tomboy, had been all her life, but in that delicate dress, she thought, she looked, well, almost pretty. "You told, Megan McQuarry," she said. "I asked you to hold your tongue, and you told Christy and Bridget about the race."

Megan blushed, though not, Skye figured, from any sense of chagrin.

"Of course she did," said Christy as she and Bridget entered the room. "We're your family. We should know these things."

"Did you really lose on purpose?" Bridget asked, lowering her voice. She might have been speaking of sacrilege.

"I most certainly did not," Skye responded, perhaps a little testily. "Except for once, when Daddy outran me on a Kentucky thoroughbred, I've never been beaten in any contest involving horses."

Megan's beautiful green eyes twinkled. "Maybe Jake Vigil is worth a little sacrifice," she suggested. "He's ever so handsome, after all, and ever so rich."

Indeed, Jake was handsome, but Skye honestly didn't care whether he had two pennies to clink together in his pants pocket. Before, she'd made him into some kind of hero, straight out of an epic and impossible tale, but now she understood that he was a flesh-and-blood man, understandably wary of women, and she loved him all the more for the person he was. Deep down, she knew that he cared for her, that one day, if she bided her time, he would come to love her truly.

Besides, he'd crossed the finish line first, hadn't he?

"You really love him," Megan said, beaming. Christy and Bridget nodded, having come, no doubt, to the same conclusion.

Shyly, Skye nodded again. She felt the heat of nettled pride rise in her cheeks all the same.

"Does he love you in return?"

Skye couldn't lie, not to her family. She and Bridget and their cousins had been brought up together on Granddaddy McQuarry's farm in Virginia. Whatever their differences, they were kin. "I don't think so," she admitted.

Megan's expression changed instantly. "Then you mustn't marry him!"

"I promised," Skye replied. Her tone said she meant it, and the look on Megan's face was one of reluctant understanding.

Bridget spoke briskly, though it seemed to Skye that her blue eyes were a little bright. "Skye knows her own mind, and she always has. If she thinks she ought to marry Jake Vigil, then she's probably right."

Megan nodded. Bridget was happily married herself, as Christy was, and she probably thought Skye and Jake's union would turn out the same way. In fact, Bridget's lack of protest gave Skye hope, for her elder sister was nobody's fool, and if she'd objected to the idea, she would have said so without hesitation and in no uncertain terms.

Megan squeezed both Skye's hands in her own. "Whatever happens," she said, "I'll be close by. You know I'd do practically anything to help you."

Skye's eyes burned with tears of affection, and she leaned forward to kiss her cousin's flawless cheek. "I know," she affirmed.

Bridget found a moment to be alone with her sister sometime later when they were about to leave for town. She held the McQuarry Bible in both hands. "I should have told you before—before your wedding day—"

Skye recalled Christy's reference to the Begats and frowned. She'd been so busy, so wrought up over the bay stallion and over Jake Vigil, that she'd forgotten. "What is it?"

"I haven't told Megan," Bridget said, by way of an answer.

Skye opened the Bible and let Bridget point out the reference she wanted her to see. Skye's face drained of color as the meaning of the inscription dawned upon her. "We're sisters?" she whispered. "But why didn't you say something?"

Bridget looked stern, then guilty, then resigned. "I guess because it's a scandal, and between our so-called fathers and mothers, this family's had enough of that."

"But why keep news like this from Megan? Christy knows, I know she does."

Bridget looked away, then looked resolutely back. "Megan is the most impulsive, the most hot-headed of all of us. It's Christy's place to tell her, and she doesn't think Megan is ready."

Skye swallowed hard and looked at the inscription again. Then a sweet, secret peace came over her, and she smiled. "It might be a scandal, but the more I think about it, the less I mind."

Bridget smiled. "Me, too," she said. "Now, let's go and get you married off, little sister."

They took a wagon and a buggy into the town of Primrose Creek, traveling in single file like a gypsy caravan. Skye rode in the buggy with Bridget and Trace, while Caney, Megan, and Christy rattled along in the wagon, Caney at the reins, Megan and Christy in the back, juggling babies and trying to keep an adventurous six-year-old Noah from pitching over the tailgate onto the hard ground.

Judge Ryan was waiting with Jake at the marshal's office, and Zachary was there, too, an amused and mischievous grin dancing in his eyes. Jake's boy, young Hank, sat on the edge of Zachary's desk, legs swinging, expression wary. Jake looked nervous enough to come out of his skin at the first sudden move on anybody's part, and Skye's heart went out to him; she forgot her own natural trepidation, at least briefly, seeing his.

Christy kissed her husband lightly, and he took their baby son, Joseph, into his arms with the ease of a man raised in a big family. Then she walked right up to Jake, looked him straight in the eye, and said, "This is right for you, Jake. I know it is."

His jaw worked as he stared down at the woman he'd loved, no doubt recalling the day just over a year before when he'd been about to marry her and she'd left him at the altar. He didn't speak, but he gave a short, brisk nod in acknowledgment.

Christy stood on tiptoe and planted a brief kiss on his lips, in the same way as and yet quite a different way from before, when she'd kissed Zachary. "Be happy," she said.

"Let's get this shindig rolling," John Ryan, the circuit judge, said gruffly, clasping a Bible in one age-gnarled hand and beckoning both bride and groom with the other. "I've got a hanging to tend to, down in Virginia City."

Skye felt in that moment as though she were mounting the steps of the gallows herself. She considered dashing for the door, ruled the option out, and took her place in front of the judge. Jake stood uneasily beside her, while Hank gamboled over to take up a manful post at his father's right hand, visibly proud of his role in the ceremony. Megan stood up for Skye, just as they'd always planned, and when Megan married, Skye would be her matron of honor.

There, in that crowded little office, amid smiling relatives and fussy babies, with a weeping prisoner looking on from the single jail cell, Jake Vigil and Skye McQuarry were wed. The whole thing was over so fast that Skye felt sure she must have let her mind wander and missed it all. She'd heard herself say "I do," though, heard Jake do the same.

It was done, and, for Skye, there was no going back.

"You go ahead, now, Jake," Judge Ryan boomed with good-natured impatience, "and kiss that pretty bride of yours!"

Jake hesitated, then took Skye's upturned face between amazingly tender hands, lifted, and brought his mouth down upon hers. It was a brief, light kiss, and yet it set Skye's very soul atremble. She realized with a thrill of delicious terror that a number of intimate mysteries would soon be revealed to her. Jake had made it plain that if they married, she would be a real wife to him, sharing his bed as well as his life.

She was still shaken when he released her, and he smiled a sweet, private smile, with only the slightest turning-up at one corner of his mouth, and sent new joy surging through her. Yes, she thought. He would come to love her. She would see to it.

At some point, Jake had slid a ring onto Skye's finger, and for the first time, she took a moment to look at it. A band set with glittering diamonds winked up at her.

"It was my mother's," Jake said, shy again.

"It's beautiful," Skye replied softly. They might

have been alone, for the others seemed far away, visible only through a dense mist.

"*You're* beautiful," he told her, and took her hand. "Shall we go home now, Mrs. Vigil, or would you rather stay here awhile with your family?"

He was family now, too, he and Hank, but she didn't trust herself not to break down and weep for foolish joy if she tried to say so aloud, so she merely nodded again.

He chuckled, and his hazel eyes were alight. "Which is it?" he prodded gently.

"Home," she managed to say. "Let's go home. But first—first, let me have a word with Hank."

Jake nodded, and Skye turned and extended a hand to her stepson. After a moment's hesitation, he accepted with his own, and she led him to one side of the room, crouching in her dress to look into his face.

"I've had some experience loving little boys," she said, "and I think you and I will get along just fine. All I need is a chance to prove myself, Hank. Will you give me that?"

He considered the question solemnly, but she saw hope in his eyes, too, far back and frightened but there. Oh, yes, it was there, all right. "I had one ma go off and leave me. I don't reckon I need another."

"I won't leave you," Skye said, and she meant it. "Not willingly."

He narrowed his eyes. "If I got the grippe in the middle of the night and called for you, would you come?"

She blinked once or twice and swallowed. Her

voice, when she spoke, was surprisingly even. "Yes," she said. "You have my word."

"Would you make me eat my vegetables all up, even if it made me sick?"

She smiled. "No," she said. "But you have to at least taste whatever I put on the table. If you don't like it, you don't have to eat it. Deal?"

Hank put out a hand again. "Deal," he said.

Five minutes later, having left the wedding in a hail of congratulations and good wishes, the bride and groom found themselves standing on the doorstep of Jake's magnificent house.

Jake scooped her up in his arms to carry her over the threshold. "The boy's spending the night with Bridget and Trace," he said. His voice, normally a baritone, seemed deeper than ever. "We'll have the place to ourselves for tonight, anyway."

Skye was looking forward to her initiation into true womanhood, for she'd long since guessed, mostly from Bridget's glowing face and tendency to sing in the mornings, and from some of her own feelings as well, that lovemaking was more than the mere duty her mother had believed it to be. Still, not knowing precisely what to expect, she was a little frightened, too.

Jake kicked the front door closed behind them. Somewhere nearby, a clock ticked in loud, measured beats, each one carrying Skye that much closer to her fate. A tangle of contradictory emotions sprang up within her. What in the name of heaven had she gotten herself into? How could she possibly bear to wait until he'd made her his own, once and for all?

He started up the grand staircase, carrying her as easily and as reverently as if she were made of the thinnest and most precious porcelain. At the top, in the hallway, he paused. A set of double doors loomed before them, slightly ajar.

"Are you scared?" He looked as though he were really concerned with her feelings, and perhaps he was. He wasn't cruel or unkind, after all. He simply didn't love her the way most new husbands loved their brides.

"A little," she confessed.

He carried her into the master bedroom, and she caught the tantalizing scents of starched linen and bay rum and of Jake himself. For the second time since they'd met, he kissed her, more deeply this time and more intensely.

The touch of his lips set her soul ablaze.

"Don't be," he said. "There are a lot of things I can't promise you, Skye. But one thing is for certain—I'll never hurt you. Not on purpose."

It was not a declaration of love, but Jake's vow brought fresh tears to Skye's eyes all the same. The contents of her own heart swelled into her throat, and only by dint of sheer desperation did she stop herself from uttering them.

Chapter

5

Jake undressed Skye slowly, reverently, like a man uncovering some sacred treasure, fold by fold. She was shy, like any virgin, however spirited, and kept her eyes lowered until he had taken away the last of her clothes. Then she looked up at him through those dark, dense lashes of hers, and he thought he glimpsed a spark of excitement there, even triumph. But he saw a certain sorrow, too. He turned her in a timeless pirouette, as though they were partners in some graceful minuet, and when her shapely back was to him, he saw the bruises.

He knew how she'd gotten them, of course—by sailing over the bay's head that morning, near the end of their race, and landing on the hard, stony ground made harder still by the long spell without rain.

Her right shoulder was the worst, purple and scraped, though her hip and one perfect buttock had sustained some damage, too. Jake was stricken by a sense of almost overwhelming tenderness, as though something infinitely precious had been marred, and he drew in his breath, closed his eyes tightly for a moment. Although he'd known he was attracted to Skye, even that he was fond of her, the depth of his emotions came as a vast and unsettling surprise.

Good God, did he love her? Had he really been stupid enough to fall into that trap for a third time in his life?

When he opened his eyes, she was facing him again, looking up into his face. "Mr. Vigil?" she asked softly.

He nearly smiled, full of passion and panic as he was. "Jake," he corrected. The word came out coarse as rusted iron, but quiet.

"You—you find me—unappealing?" she asked, and that look of personal misery was back in her eyes.

"No," he rasped quickly. "God, no. It's just—I should have realized—"

She frowned, still confused.

"That you were hurt. When you were thrown this morning."

Her smile was sudden and dazzling. "Oh," she said. "That. Well—er, Jake—that wasn't the first spill I've taken from a horse, and I'm pretty sure it won't be the last."

She did not seem to realize how delicate she looked to him. He felt big as a grizzly bear, awkward and inept, faced with this lovely, trusting, porcelain creature, and all the tumbles he'd taken with various local prostitutes meant nothing, in terms of experience, faced with the prospect of bedding an innocent young bride.

Cautiously, he lifted his right arm and ran the backs of his fingers down the length of her arm, shoulder to wrist, barely touching her yet eliciting a shiver. He was instantly alarmed, seized with an urge to swaddle her in quilts, like an invalid.

"Are you cold?"

She smiled a mysterious woman-smile and shook her head.

"You seem so small," he confessed.

She held his gaze intrepidly. "Well," she said, "I'm not. In fact, I'm tall for a woman. Everyone's always said so."

He thought of the bruises again. "I wouldn't want to—to hurt you."

Her eyes softened. They were like velvet as it was, those eyes, brown and rich, drawing him in, laying permanent claim to his soul. "I don't know much of anything about this," she said, and blushed a little, "except what I've seen animals do."

Maybe it was nerves that made him grin. "It's a little different with people," he said. He felt the grin fade from his face, replaced by consternation. "I reckon it might hurt, just a little, this first time."

She nodded. "Bridget told me that," she said.

"Ahh," Jake replied. Somehow, without his knowing, his hands had come to rest on the smooth, nearly imperceptible slope of her shoulders, and the pads of his thumbs made slow circles in the hollows above her collarbone. He didn't dare look at her breasts again; he was at the ragged edge of his self-control as it was, and he wasn't sure how long he could restrain himself if he were to see the nipples tighten under his gaze.

She raised her chin and carried on the conversation with the special aplomb that is woman's alone. "After that," she said, "I won't mind."

He wanted so much more for her than "not minding," when it came to his physical attentions, but he was dealing with a new bride, he reminded himself. Such things took time and skill, tenderness and patience. Jake had all those qualities, though he would have been the first to admit that the latter was a bit taxed at the moment. If she'd been one of the loose women over at Diamond Lil's, he'd probably be putting his shirt back on by now, but she wasn't. Dear God, she wasn't.

He swallowed hard and hoped she didn't guess that he was nervous, too. One of them, it seemed to him, ought to be in charge.

"Don't you think you should undress?" she asked logically. "After all, I'm standing here naked, and there you are, wearing everything but a hat."

He felt heat surge into his face at the idea of taking off his clothes in front of this delectable little nymph—God, he might have been an uninitiated youth instead of a man with a long and rather colorful history behind him. Reluctantly, he removed his suit coat, loosened his tie.

A groan escaped him when she pushed his hands gently aside and began to unfasten the buttons of his shirt, and the sound must have pleased her, for her dark eyes were shining as she looked up at him, her fingers busy all the while.

"I'll be a good wife to you, Jake Vigil," she said.

He kissed her then, suddenly, and with a lot of force, surprising both of them. When it was over and he'd recovered enough strength to draw his head back and look at her, he saw a bedazzled expression in her eyes. He wished he could tell her he loved her, wished it sorely, but for all his wanting, for all his passion, he knew there was a void inside him where tender sentiments should be. A place that had to be kept closed off.

"I'll protect you," he said gruffly, "and I'll always provide. No matter what."

She didn't respond but simply pushed his shirt back over his shoulders. He shed the garment, let it fall unheeded to the floor. Within a few seconds, he, too, was stripped to the skin.

He had no recollection of taking her to the bed, tossing back the covers, sprawling next to her on the smooth linen sheets. He was in a fever, a delirium, and by the time his mind cleared, even a little, they were lying on their sides, facing each other, the skin of their thighs touching. He rested a hand on the supple curve of her hip.

"Don't be afraid," she said.

Under any other circumstances, that remark would have amused him, but there, in his bed, with his brand new wife awaiting him like a feast, he was touched instead. He ran the tip of one index finger lightly from her temple to her chin, then traced the shape of her delectable mouth. The next thing he knew, he was kissing her again, and so desperate to be inside her that it took all his self-control to keep from mounting her right then.

Instead, he took his time, introducing her to every nuance of pleasure—rousing soft cries from her when he grasped her wrists together, above her head, and suckled at her breasts, sometimes leisurely, sometimes with the hunger that was already consuming him, sending the blood racing hot through his veins.

He reached her silken belly in due time and made a circle around her navel with the tip of his tongue. When he did that, she gasped and arched her back, raising herself to him like an offering. Instinct had taken over Skye's every action and movement.

Knowing that, he was lost.

He moved down, beneath the quilts and the top sheet, and slid his hands under her buttocks, lifted her to his mouth like a chalice. When she felt his tongue, quickly followed by the tugging of his lips, she sobbed his name, plunged her fingers into his hair, and begged.

He could not deny her but drew on her with more insistence, and still more, until her excitement had turned to frenzy and her buttocks were quivering in his hands. When, at long last, she stiffened against him, moist and flexing, he called upon the last dregs of personal discipline to guide her over every peak. Finally, when she sagged, sighing raggedly, to the mattress, he parted her legs gently and poised himself above her.

"Skye?" He was asking her permission, and she knew it.

She looked up at him dreamily, blinking, and a silly, beautiful smile curved her kiss-swollen mouth. "Yes," she said on a breath. "Oh, yes."

He found her entrance, slid slowly inside her. He felt the maidenhead give way, and though she flinched a little as he breached that last barrier, her breathing soon quickened, and her hips began to move in precise rhythm with his.

He was amazed.

"Oh," she whispered. "Oh, Jake——"

"Shh." He kissed her, his tongue sparring with hers.

She began to buck beneath him, fitfully at first and then with an age-old eagerness. He rode her, plunging deep, covering her face, her jaw, her neck with kisses as they rose and fell together.

And then, for Jake Vigil at least, the universe exploded, spewing stars. At the same time, Skye clung to him, her fingernails deep in the flesh of his back, and cried out in satisfaction, over and over again.

She lay still beneath him, sated, swept away, and utterly embarrassed by the echoes of her own abandon. Nothing, *nothing* Skye had ever heard, read, or imagined about the act of love had prepared her for the reality—for the fever, the need, the tender violence of it. Her throat was raw, and she was mortified, thinking she must surely have shouted right out loud in her frantic jubilance. She knew by the twisted sheets and the cool sheen of perspiration on her skin that she had been thrashing about, and she turned her face to one side.

Jake, still breathing hard, lay balanced on his thighs and forearms, careful not to crush her. "Skye," he said, and though the word was gentle, there was a command in it. "Look at me."

She looked, cheeks flaming. She'd *shouted,* she agonized silently. She'd tossed back and forth and up and down on the bed like a shameless hussy. What must he think of her?

"What," he demanded quietly, "is going on in that mind of yours?"

She lowered her lashes, and he kissed each of her eyelids, ever so softly. The warmth of his lips sent a hot thrill of fresh, unexpected fire through her, stealing her breath. She gasped and met his gaze again, her heart picking up speed like a steam engine chugging downhill. "I was just—just wondering—I mean, I've never—I'm just not sure—"

He smiled and kissed the tip of her nose. "Let's just say I'm glad you lost that horse race this morning," he said, with mischief dancing in his eyes.

Skye was glad, too, but she wasn't so far gone as to admit it. She didn't want Jake to start thinking she'd taken that spill intentionally, because she hadn't. At least, she was pretty sure she hadn't.

"I'm sorry we can't take a honeymoon trip," he said, and he looked for all the world as though he meant it. Skye was seeing a side of Jake she had never glimpsed before, as deeply as she had loved him; behind all that strength and power and obstinance lurked a passionate, skillful lover, a poet, not of pretty phrases but of caresses and kisses and whispered urgings. "Not just yet, anyhow." He rolled onto his back beside her and sighed, gazing up at the ceiling. "You might as well know, you've married a man who might just lose every cent."

She raised herself onto one elbow and peered down into his face. He was magnificent, lying there, broad at the shoulders and deep through the chest, his hair still mussed from her fingers and his aristocratic features at peace in a way she had never known them to be. It gave her a delicious sense of power to know that she'd done this for him, however unwittingly, that she'd given him the singular, womanly solace of her body.

"I don't care," she said. "If you go broke, I mean. We can live on my land."

She saw amazement in his eyes as he stared at her. "You don't care?" He sounded as though he couldn't believe what he was hearing.

"Well," she allowed, finding the strength at last to sit up, pulling the sheets modestly up over her breasts. "Of course I care. I mean, you've worked hard for all this. But it doesn't really change the important things, does it? We still have each other, and Hank. We're a family now. We have my sister and my cousins and the land at Primrose Creek."

He smiled and tugged the sheet down, smiled again when she blushed. "You, Mrs. Vigil," he said, "are a remarkable woman." He traced the circumference of a nipple with the tip of one finger, delighting in the instinctive response and the little groan Skye couldn't hold back. "Come here," he said, drawing her down into his embrace. "Let me show you just *how* remarkable."

She was lost then, utterly, completely, triumphantly lost. And, for the moment at least, she didn't give a tinker's damn about being found.

Hank stood watching Skye from the doorway of Jake's enormous kitchen one morning, some three days following the wedding, and the expression in his eyes was at once cautious and hopeful. "I didn't figure on gettin' myself another ma," he said. "Fact is, the one I had wasn't much."

Skye, who had been assessing the contents of the pantry, which were sorry indeed, wiped her hands on the apron she'd fashioned from a dishtowel and smiled down at the little boy. He'd avoided her neatly so far, except for their brief exchange after the wedding, but now he evidently felt ready to draw up some kind of unwritten treaty. He was the very image of Jake; when he grew to be a man, she expected he'd look much the way his father did now. "I see," she said carefully, keeping her distance lest she frighten the child away. He reminded her of a yearling deer, curious but watchful, too. Prepared to spring away into the underbrush at the slightest provocation. Her tone was thoughtful, almost bemused. "Well, I didn't precisely expect to get a little boy, either. At least, not right away. All the same, I'm really, truly glad I did."

"I'm *not* a little boy," Hank protested.

Skye bit back a smile. "No," she said with a

ponderous shake of her head. "I don't suppose you are."

"I don't have to do what you tell me."

She dragged a chair back from the round oak table, sat down, and propped her chin in her hands. "I'm not entirely sure that's true," she said. "I do expect you to wash behind your ears and keep your teeth clean and, of course, to do your chores and schoolwork."

He made a face. "Women," he scoffed.

Skye wanted to laugh, but somehow she managed to maintain a properly serious expression. "I think we can learn to be friends if we really try."

"But you're not my ma." He plainly wanted that understood.

Jake had told Skye what little he knew about his son's past. She wondered what sort of a woman gave birth to a child, kept his existence a secret from the man who'd fathered him, and then abandoned that same child with little or no compunction. Her heart went out to Hank, though she was careful not to reveal that, either. Long experience with Noah had taught her to communicate with children as persons in their own right.

"No, I'm not your mother," she allowed. "That's true. But I would certainly be proud if you were my son."

The hazel eyes widened, narrowed again. "You're just sayin' that," he accused.

She shook her head. "Absolutely not. I never say things I don't mean. Do you?"

He studied her in silence for a long while, and she

waited, content to let him speak when and if he was ready. "Sometimes," he admitted. "Sometimes I tell lies."

Skye kept her features very grave. "Oh."

"And sometimes I spit."

She nodded solemnly.

"And if I don't care for a place, then I just move on."

"Hmmm," Skye said. "Well, I hope you'll like Primrose Creek and stay right here with us. I think your father would be very disappointed if you left."

Hank's small, freckled brow furrowed briefly. "What about you? Would you be sad? If I lit out, I mean?"

"Oh, yes," she answered. "You see, we're going to have some babies around here, and they'll need an older brother to watch out for them. Oh, they'll have their cousin Noah, of course, and eventually the others will be big enough to help out, too, but that won't be the same as having a real brother, right there under the same roof and everything."

Hank looked pensive and a bit torn. Eagerness sparked in his eyes, though she knew he was doing his best to suppress the emotion. Poor, sweet thing; heaven only knew what sort of tribulations he'd gone through before coming to Primrose Creek. No wonder he was such a stalwart and serious little man.

"Did you marry my pa so's you could live in this fancy house?"

The question caught Skye off-guard and stung smartly. She hadn't married Jake for any reason other than love, though she wasn't about to explain her most intimate feelings to a seven-year-old. Jake, on the contrary, and despite his many protestations, had almost certainly married her for the timber on her land, though she didn't doubt that he regarded her highly. A man as handsome, as capable, as downright *good* as Jake Vigil could have had his pick of women.

She decided to ignore the inquiry entirely, since she'd already left it dangling so long. "There isn't much in the pantry," she said, getting back to her feet with a sigh of resolution, "but I've managed to scrape up some oatmeal and molasses. Come have your breakfast. You mustn't be late for school."

"I hate school," he said, dragging his feet as he approached the table.

Skye went to the stove, busied herself with stirring and scooping, as she'd seen Bridget do a thousand times. It was strange how such simple tasks as cooking oatmeal and looking after a child could give a person so much joy. "Well, you'll need schooling," she said, "if you hope to follow in your father's footsteps. He's a very intelligent man, you know. You've seen all his books on the shelves in the study? He must have hundreds, and it looks to me as if he's read them all—"

Hank made a great deal of noise getting into a chair and situating himself just so at the table. "Noah says you're all right," he said. "So I reckon I'll stay put awhile."

She hid a smile.

"He's about to go under, my pa," the child confided. "That's what they say at school. Then he won't want me underfoot no more. He probably won't want you, neither."

Skye was careful not to meet Hank's gaze for a few moments, for her own was glittering with a sheen of tears, quickly blinked away. "Your father will *never* give you away," she said, and it was in that moment the one thing she was truly sure of. "Never."

It was more than a rumor, though, the reference to Jake's financial situation. He'd admitted that to her himself the day they were married. She hadn't minded then, except for his sake, anyway, and she didn't now. She had land, she had timber, she had the gold that sifted down out of the mountains, settling like silt in the creek bed. She had strength and love and competence, and if she couldn't build a life from those things, she was just plain useless.

Skye set the bowl of steaming oatmeal, generously laced with molasses, before him. "Don't you go worrying, now. Your father's not beaten yet. And even if he was, why, we could start over, the three of us, just by pushing up our sleeves and getting down to work."

He looked at her for a long, poignant moment. "Their pas work for my pa, mostly. The kids at school, I mean. Everybody's real scared."

Skye dared to stroke the boy's hair, and, to her surprise, he did not pull away. For the first time, it came to her how high-handed she'd been in the beginning, flatly refusing to sell her timber to Jake or anyone else.

She'd never once thought how many people would be affected by her rather blithe decision, and now she was ashamed.

Hank's words echoed in her ears all morning. *Everybody's real scared.*

Jake came home at around noon and found her in the study, with leather-bound volumes in teetering piles all around her. He looked harried and quite unsure of his welcome, but he smiled when he saw her, as though there were something amusing about a woman sorting books.

His clothes were covered with dirt, and his hair was full of sawdust, but Skye didn't care. When he pulled her close, her senses arose as one and spun their way upward in a whirlwind of sparks, like ghost leaves rising from a garden fire. He brushed a smudge from her cheek with the pad of one thumb and kissed her forehead.

"My wife," he said, as though he could not believe his good fortune.

Skye's throat closed, so great was the swell of emotion that arose within her, and some moments had passed before she managed to speak. "About the timber—" she began.

He laid an index finger to her lips. It was a gentle gesture, intended to soothe, no doubt, but it had exactly the opposite effect on Skye. She was dancing with lightning; if Jake had carried her upstairs to their bedroom, she would have gone willingly, even though it was the middle of the day.

"Never mind the timber," he said.

She blinked. "But it's yours now, at least partly—"

He interrupted with a shake of his head. "No," he said in a firm voice, and held her away from him. It was a minor distance—his hands were still cupping her elbows—but Skye felt it sorely. "The land, those trees—all of that's yours. And I know how much those trees mean to you."

Skye was speechless. Jubilance and confusion tussled within her.

"I'm the head of this household," he went on solemnly, "and I'll pay my debts and provide for my wife and child. Somehow."

"You're just being stubborn, Jake Vigil," she accused when she found the breath to speak. "You *need* that timber."

He withdrew further just then; she felt it, even though she would have sworn he hadn't actually moved. "No," he said. "What I need is to be able to look at my face in the mirror every morning when I shave without being tempted to turn away in disgust. If you want to back out—"

Skye's eyes widened, and her mouth dropped open. She had to close it again consciously. When she spoke, she was trembling with controlled fury. "Are you suggesting that I back out of this marriage? Just go home to Primrose Creek and pretend nothing's changed?"

He heaved a sigh. "Only if you want to," he said.

She stared at him. "Well," she told him, "I don't. I'm not some throwaway woman, Jake Vigil. I'm a wife, and I mean to stay that way!"

He grinned, his white teeth making a startling contrast with his dirty, rascally face. "You lost that race on purpose."

She stomped one foot. "I did not!"

He laughed. "Yes," he pressed, frankly enjoying her high dudgeon. "I think maybe you did. You *wanted* to marry me."

She *had* wanted to marry Jake, she was crazy about him, and she had been for a long time, but she would have won that race if she could have, would have left Jake Vigil and his second-rate stallion choking in the dust! With huffy little motions, she smoothed her hair, straightened her spine, dusted her hands together. "I've made cheese potatoes," she said. "For your dinner."

"Admit it," he said. "You wanted to marry me."

"All right," she said. "It's true."

He grinned and folded his arms. "Why?"

"Because I wanted lumber for a house," she lied.

He laughed. "Try again."

She flushed. "Because—I wanted—babies."

In a single motion, he swept her up into his arms.

"What about dinner?" she asked, her heart thrumming at the back of her throat.

He kissed her forehead, then bent to nip lightly at one of her breasts. "I'm not interested in dinner," he said, and started up the stairs.

The man at the Western Union office read the telegram Skye had written out and peered at her through greasy spectacles. He was a doddering old fellow, and his jaw shook with effort while he rallied his powers of speech. "This here is to the vice president of the railroad, Mrs. Vigil," he said.

She leaned forward and spoke in a cheerful whisper. "I know that," she said. "After all, I wrote it."

He was still skeptical. "You talked this over with Jake, I reckon?"

"I do not recall asking for your counsel in this matter or any other, Mr. Abbot," Skye pointed out. "That timber is mine, after all, and if I want to sell it to the railroad, I jolly well will. Furthermore, if you mention this to my husband, I will know you betrayed a confidence and report you to the Western Union people." Maybe Jake was willing to let go of everything he'd worked for by turning his back on a lot of perfectly good timber, but she wasn't about to let him. She'd sell the trees herself if he refused to do so, and the railroad would be forced to let Jake cut the ties for the tracks, since there wasn't another mill within miles, thereby fulfilling his contract.

Mr. Abbot blinked. "That beats all," he said, but he sounded subdued. Skye hadn't expected him to be the least bit daunted by her threat, since it was largely an empty one, but apparently he had taken it to heart. "Don't know what the world's coming to, when a new bride'll steal business from her own husband—"

"I'll find out," Skye warned ominously, probably overplaying her hand a little but emboldened by her success in buffaloing Mr. Abbot, "if you tell." With that, she counted out the fee for sending the wire, slapping each coin down onto the counter with a little flourish, and waited obstinately while Mr. Abbot

tapped out the words that would change everything—for better or for worse.

Megan came to call first thing the next morning
and took in the wonders of Jake's house with amazement. The last time Megan or any of them had been
inside the mansion, Jake had been courting Christy.
He'd ordered all sorts of fancy furnishings to please
her back then, things it looked as though no one had
touched since.

"This is even bigger than Granddaddy's place,"
Megan said when she and Skye were seated in the
great, echoing parlor, sipping tea.

"Umm," Skye replied. The house seemed cold and
imposing, and she would have preferred to live on
Primrose Creek, with Jake and young Hank, of
course, in the simpler place she'd planned so carefully
in her mind. "That was different," she said at some
length. "The farm, I mean. That house was always
brimming with noise and music and—well—*life*.
This place is like a museum."

Megan looked impish. "Are you complaining,
Skye McQuarry Vigil? If so, I must say that you lack
conviction—your eyes sparkle, and your skin glows.
You look like you're going to start singing for joy at
any moment." She lowered her voice and leaned forward in her velvet chair. "Is it wonderful? Being married, I mean?"

"Married?" Skye echoed, a little stupidly.

"You know," Megan persisted. *"Married."*

Color throbbed in Skye's face. "Oh," she said.

Megan would not let the subject go. "Well?"

"Yes," Skye admitted in an embarrassed rush, unable to keep herself from beaming. "And don't ask me to tell you any more, because I positively will not, Megan McQuarry."

Megan settled back, grinning. "I wouldn't dream of prying," she lied. Prying was her calling in life.

Just then, Hank burst through the front door and appeared in the parlor doorway. His eyes were enormous, and there was no color in his face at all. "There's a fire comin'!" he yelled.

For Skye, everything stopped for a moment, the world, time itself, even her heartbeat. It was the thing they had most feared, all of them, and it had come upon them. "*What?*"

"Pa sent me to tell you Mr. Hicks is comin' with a wagon. We're supposed to pack up whatever we can and head for the low country—"

Skye and Megan were both on their feet in an instant, racing toward the front door. They reached it at the same time and stared in horror at the rim of black, roiling smoke surging along the western horizon. The blaze was big, and though it was still far away, it looked as if it was headed straight for Primrose Creek.

"I'll be needed at home," Megan cried, and dashed down the walk to mount Speckles, the mare she'd left tethered to the fence. She didn't bother with decorum but planted one foot in the stirrup, swung the other leg over the saddle, and rode astride.

Skye thought anxiously of Bridget and Trace, of

Noah and the twins and all the horses and cattle, but unlike Megan, she did not bolt for the homestead. She was a married woman now, responsible for a child, and if she'd gone flying off to help her sister and cousins, Bridget would have been the first to tell her to go home and look after her own.

She turned quickly and smoothed Hank's hair back from his worried face. "Where is your pa? Over at the mill?"

Hank nodded vigorously. "We'd better get movin'," he said. "Pa said he'd whup me good if I didn't mind him, 'cause there's no time to waste!"

The acrid scent of smoke reached Skye then, souring the spring breeze that had made the earlier part of the day so pleasant. Tears burned in her eyes. Perhaps it wouldn't matter now, that she'd gone behind Jake's back and offered to sell the timber on her land to the railroad. If that fire kept traveling in the same direction, there wouldn't *be* any timber.

"You go into the parlor," she said calmly, laying a hand on Hank's skinny little shoulder, "and gather as many of the books together as you can. I'll fetch blankets and food."

Hank nodded and raced toward his father's study. If he questioned the wisdom of saving books instead of other, more practical items, such as chairs and washtubs, pots and pans and butter churns, he didn't say so.

Mr. Hicks appeared with the wagon only minutes later, and, as the air grew thicker and sootier and more difficult to breathe, Skye wondered with real despair if all of Nevada was on fire. Still, she raced back and forth, helping to load the wagon. When it was full, she urged Hank up into the box and turned toward the mill, searching through the billowing smoke for her husband.

Jake was striding across the road, and, reaching her, he took her by the shoulders and kept on going, shuffling her along with him, until they were beside the wagon. "Head down the mountain, Skye," he rasped. "Go as far as you can tonight. I'll look for you at Fort Grant first, and if I don't find you there, I'll come to Virginia City."

Skye was horrified. It had not occurred to her that she and Hank would be leaving without Jake. It was unthinkable—they were a family, the three of them. They belonged together, no matter what.

He must have read her thoughts, for before she could speak, Jake put a finger under her chin and lifted, closing her mouth. "For once in your life," he said, "don't argue with me. This whole mountain could go up if we don't stop that fire. All the men are staying to fight it, and, frankly, we don't need anything else to worry about!"

She looked around, saw for the first time in her panic that the road was already thick with fleeing wagons and buckboards. Where, she wondered desperately, were Bridget and her children? What of Christy and the new baby, little Joseph? What would happen to the houses, the barns, the livestock?

Jake hoisted her into the wagon. "Go," he said.

She gazed down at him for a long moment, loving

him, but unable to say it, even then, for fear he would turn away. "I'll be back," she said. "Once Hank is safe at Fort Grant, I'm coming straight back."

"Don't you dare," Jake warned. His jawline looked hard, and she knew he wasn't fooling. "I mean it, Skye."

She took up the reins. "So do I," she answered, and guided the wagon around in a wide arc, joining the exodus from Primrose Creek.

As a McQuarry, Skye was possessed of many singular characteristics, but a propensity for blind obedience did not number among them. Her intentions were as firmly set as her jawline while she drove the team and wagon ever further, ever faster, away from nearly everyone and everything she held dear. She would go back. As soon as she could, she would return to Primrose Creek and battle the fire herself, hand-to-hand. After all, she had as much to lose as anybody else.

Smoke chased the noisy band of scrambling escapees, rolling over them like some dark, acrid tide, causing Skye's eyes to burn, as dry as if she'd opened the door of a blast furnace and peeked inside. It was hard to see the road, harder still to breathe. Deer sprang alongside the track now and then, fleeing the flames, and small animals—squirrels, raccoons, and rabbits mostly—scampered in the ruts and in the ditches, their high-pitched squeals adding to the din.

Beside her in the wagon box, Hank crouched on the floor, with Mr. Hicks's bandanna pressed to his face. His eyes were enormous with fright as he looked up at Skye, his knuckles white where he gripped the seat with one hand and the side of the box with the other.

Hurry, urged the voice of instinct, *hurry.* And Skye listened. She stood, reins in hand, feet set to hold her balance, and drove the already-lathered team harder, and then harder yet. Squinting through the smoke, when she dared to look away from the road ahead, Skye glimpsed Bridget and Christy in a shared wagon, comforting the smaller children in the back while Caney held the traces, traveling at a pace to rival Skye's own. Megan rode alongside on her spirited mare, with Noah behind her, his little arms clenched tightly around her middle.

Noah had always been Skye's special charge, and her heart went out to her nephew, finding its way through the smoke and soot and fear. He must have felt her regard, for he turned his head immediately, and their eyes connected.

She smiled at him, willing him to know that she thought he was being very, very brave.

Skye did not know how far they'd traveled, the McQuarry women and their various charges, the townswomen and theirs, when they were met by a large contingent of cavalrymen from Fort Grant. Uniforms already stained with soot, prepared for a fight that might well mean life or death to some of them, as to a great many secret and cherished dreams hiding in the hearts of all these terrified but determined women and children, Skye thought those soldiers were among the most splendid sights she'd ever seen.

They had outrun the smoke, she and the others, and while the fort was still a long way off, Skye at last could see the walls and watchtowers from her place in the wagon box. She drew back on the reins with all her might and still barely stopped the four-horse team. Caney brought the other rig to an able halt beside her.

"I'm going to unhitch one of these horses and ride back!" Skye called to her, and coughed. "Megan can turn the mare loose and drive the wagon the rest of the way—"

Caney's eyes flashed with temper and resolve. "You ain't goin' nowhere, missy, so you can just put *that* dern fool idea right out of your head! You a mama to that little boy now, and you cain't leave him!"

She risked a glance down at Hank and found him looking plaintively back up at her. Caney was right, she reflected, but ruefully. She hadn't even known he existed until just a few days before, but Hank was hers all the same, born of her heart if not of her body. She loved him with a sudden and primitive fierceness that was startling to recognize; this, she knew, was the way her granddaddy, Gideon McQuarry, had loved her and Bridget, Christy, and Megan. It was a gift, that kind of commitment to another person, for the lover as well as the beloved, and more important than anything else on earth.

She sat down in the wagon seat, holding the reins loosely in one hand, and ruffled her stepson's hair. "I'm staying," she said simply, and soon, while the cavalry hurried toward Primrose Creek, at least a hundred strong, she and Caney and the others once again set out for the fort itself.

There, they were given quarters in one of the barracks, a long, spacious room cleared especially for them and lined on either side with metal cots. A hot and restorative—if not particularly tasty—meal was served in the mess hall, and Bridget and Christy took informal command of the situation, supervising the collecting and washing of dishes, mugs, and utensils. By nightfall, the other women of the town and its surrounding area were settled in, hopeful if still subdued, resigned to looking after the children and waiting for their men to come and fetch them.

Once the meal was over, though, and the various children of the family had been bedded down, Skye was restless. After making sure Hank was asleep in the cot next to the one she'd claimed for herself, she went outside under a starry spring sky.

She stood looking up for a long moment, the smell of smoke still rife in her hair and the folds of her clothes, even on her skin, and prayed that whatever happened to the land, the timber, and the town, the people up there in the high country would be kept safe. Jake's image filled her mind and brought stinging tears to her eyes. He could so easily be killed, burned or crushed beneath a falling tree or building, or simply overcome by smoke. He was her husband,

and though he had laid skillful claim to her body on more than one occasion, she had never told him that she loved him with all her heart and soul, as well as her flesh. Her silly, stubborn pride had gotten in the way, and now she might never have a chance to make things right.

Despondently, she climbed a stairway to one of the parapets, where she met and passed one of several young soldiers making his rounds.

The place she knew as Primrose Creek, the place she knew as home, glowed bright crimson against a background of darkness. Perhaps it was gone, all of it, even then—the home Bridget and Trace had built with love and hard work, the Indian lodge Christy and Zachary had transformed into a haven. The timber and animals on her portion of land and on Megan's. The tents and shacks and saloons, the sawmill, and Jake's grand monstrosity of a house. She closed her eyes against all those images of destruction, told herself that everything would be all right. They would survive, all of them, and rebuild as best they could. In time, the forest animals would return, and the trees would grow again.

A whisper of sound at her right side brought Skye back to the moment. She turned to see Christy standing there, a shawl pulled tightly around her slender shoulders. Although she had just given birth a few days before, and she was clearly tired, Christy's backbone was McQuarry-straight, and her chin was high as she followed Skye's gaze.

"It's the hardest thing in the world," Skye's cousin mused, "not being there with Zachary."

Skye nodded. "I can't stop thinking about Jake," she agreed.

Christy sighed. She'd wound her heavy dark hair in a bun at her nape, and it was slipping its pins, ready to tumble down her back, but she seemed heedless of everything but that distant fire and the man she loved, up there fighting the blaze with the rest of the men. "I'd give a lot to be there right now. To know Zachary and the others are all right. Bridget's frantic over Trace, too, though she doesn't think anyone can tell."

Skye smiled at the mention of her sister. Bridget was the McQuarry-est of McQuarrys. She had their granddaddy's indomitable spirit, and what she lacked in physical stature she made up in grit and intelligence. She was a wildcat at heart, Bridget was, equal to any challenge, and it was a sure bet that if she hadn't had the twins and Noah to care for, she'd have been at her husband's side at that very moment. "Don't you worry about Bridget," she said, and then touched her cousin's shoulder lightly, remembering her cousin's anxiety when the baby was about to be born and Zachary was nowhere to be found. "But what about you, Christy? Are you all right?"

Christy hesitated for only the merest fraction of a beat before nodding. "Yes," she said, her attention still fixed on the distant fire. Even from so far away, the blaze cast a moving reflection over Christy's perfect features. "A person can lose all they have, so quickly—"

There was certainly no way to refute that statement, it was patently true, but Skye slipped her arm around Christy and gave her a brief, reassuring squeeze anyway. All four of the Primrose Creek women had known tremendous loss in recent years. The farm that had nurtured them all was gone forever. Their grandmother had passed on, then their fathers and mothers, and eventually, and most grievous of all, they'd had to say good-bye to their beloved grandfather, the cornerstone of their lives. Bridget had seen a young husband march off to war, only to return in a pinewood box. Of them all, though, it often seemed to Skye that Christy always had been the most sensitive and thus the most easily wounded; she was surely thinking of Zachary again, and of what it would mean to lose him.

"We had each other, Christy. You and me and Bridget and Megan. And Caney, too." She paused, thinking of the family Bible and the secret it contained. "Surely you'll tell Megan now? About the four of us being sisters?"

Christy shook her head, then sighed philosophically and worked up a faltering smile. That was Christy for you; she was temperamental, proud, and stubborn as a mule belly-deep in mud, but she was also one of the most courageous people Skye had ever known. None knew better than Bridget, Megan, Caney, and Skye herself how afraid Christy had been of giving her heart to Zachary, lest it be broken, but she'd gone ahead and done it anyway, and she'd been happy as a result. Through it all, she still wanted to protect her little sister.

"Everything's happened so fast," Christy said,

brushing a lock of smoke-scented hair back from Skye's forehead. "I didn't get a chance."

"She deserves to know."

Christy's eyes filled with tears. "It will break her heart."

"Why?"

"She thought the sun rose and set on Granddaddy. When she finds out he lied all those years—"

"He wanted to protect all of us."

"Maybe," Christy said. "And maybe he just wanted to protect his son, the worst scoundrel of all, your—our—father." She sighed again. "I must confess, though, it's something of a relief to know Jenny wasn't Megan's and my mother. She didn't love us very much, and we always thought it was some fault in ourselves."

"Did Caney know?" Skye asked gently.

"Oh, yes," Christy replied. "Of course she did. In fact, when our dear daddy's lovely mistress came to term with each one of us, Caney was there to attend to the matter and see that no tales were spread. It was Granddaddy who gave two of us to each of his remaining sons and Granddaddy who insisted that we all grow up believing we'd been born to the parents he'd assigned us."

"I wonder what Grandmother thought."

Christy gave a chuckle that was utterly without humor. "Granddaddy loved her to distraction, but when it came to serious matters like a firstborn son so intolerable that they paid him to leave home and stay away, his word was law."

Skye nodded. "Bridget didn't tell me his name. Our father's, I mean."

"Thayer," Christy said in a faraway and very weary voice. "He was named for our great-grandfather. What a disappointment he must have been to Granddaddy and Grandmother!"

"It's odd that no one ever mentioned him, that there wasn't a portrait or a letter—"

"He was what the English call a remittance man. Granddaddy gave him his inheritance and sent him away when he was still very young."

"We had different mothers, though." Bridget had told her that much, though she hadn't been entirely forthcoming where the family scandal was concerned.

"How do you know that?"

Once again, Christy sighed. "Granddaddy left a letter. It was written on thin paper and tucked beneath the lining of the back cover on the Bible."

Skye let out her breath, feeling a little angry herself now. Bridget and Christy, being the oldest, had naturally thought they knew best, but they had been wrong to keep the secret as long as they had. Skye and Megan were not children, and they had a right to know who they were.

"I see," she said.

Christy squeezed her hand. "I'm not sure you do. There's more, Skye."

Skye braced herself, sensing that this last bit of news would be the most startling of all. "Tell me," she insisted. When she saw Bridget again, she would tell her off three ways from Sunday for hiding so much from her.

But Christy said nothing more. She merely resumed her vigil, gazing toward the fire and waiting for Zachary. Plainly, for that night at least, the subject was closed.

The heat and glare of the fire were nearly unbearable, and Jake watched with hot, itching eyes as the roof of his mansion fell in, sending a shower of sparks and flames shooting toward the smoke-shrouded sky. The mill was gone, and so was most of the rest of the town—only the marshal's office, that pitiful shack of a schoolhouse, and Diamond Lil's saloon were still standing.

Someone slapped him on the shoulder. "The worst is over," a voice said. "The fire's turning back on itself."

He recognized Trace Qualtrough, though it was God's own wonder that he could, for the man was black with soot from the top of his head to the soles of his boots. The whites of his eyes stood out, and when he smiled, Jake actually blinked at the brightness of his teeth.

"You reckon the women are all right?" he asked.

Trace nodded. "Yep."

"Your place—at Primrose Creek?"

Trace ran a forearm across his brow, and afterward he was as dirty as before. "I've been on the mountain most of the day, but Zachary rode out home as soon as we could spare him. Says everything's still standing."

He had the good grace to look a little chagrined, Trace did, though Jake wasn't precisely sure how he'd been able to discern the fact, given all that soot. "You still have Skye, and the land, and her timber," Trace said, more gently. "A man's got a McQuarry woman at his side, he can do anything."

Jake thrust a hand through his hair and looked around behind him. He couldn't talk about Skye just now, couldn't even bear to think about her. It was as if he would somehow jinx her if he let her into his mind, and she and the boy would be in greater danger than they already were. "Anybody hurt?"

"Mike Finn is in a pretty bad way," Trace answered solemnly. "Reckon he breathed in too much smoke. And Malcolm's got some nasty burns on his right arm."

"They're being tended to?"

Again, Trace nodded. "Captain Tatum came up with the troops. He does the doctoring down at Fort Grant." He sighed. "There's already some talk about giving up on this town, starting over someplace else. You wouldn't be thinking along those lines, would you, Jake?"

There were folks who said Trace Qualtrough could get inside a horse's head and read its mind. Just then, Jake wondered if the man possessed the same uncanny skill where human beings were concerned. "Either way," he said, "we'll have to start over. Might as well be here as anyplace else."

Trace grinned, pleased, and slapped Jake's shoulder again. Ashes rose from the fabric of his shirt. "Might as well," he agreed.

That night, when the last blazes were out, men took turns standing watch, lest the few remaining buildings be consumed. Jake let himself be persuaded to ride out to the Qualtrough place, where he took a bath in the creek and slept in the bed that had been Skye's before they were married. The scent of her skin and hair lingered in the linens, and, comforted, he fell into an immediate, consuming sleep.

Despite the old adage that things usually look better in the morning, the plain light of day had a sobering effect on just about everybody. Most of the horses and cattle had been turned loose as the fire drew nearer, so they'd have at least a chance of escaping the heat, flames, and smoke; now, those that had survived would have to be rounded up again. Newly planted crops were either burned or blanketed in ash, and a thousand trees, most of them on Jake's own land, loomed black and brittle and spindly-limbed against the sky.

Jake had managed to keep the bay stallion tethered in the schoolyard with a few others, when the livestock was scattered to the four winds, and that morning he was glad, for, by his reckoning, the bay was all he had left—when it came to material things, anyway. Skye and Hank were safe at Fort Grant or in Virginia City, and that mattered more than anything else.

The town, when he reached it, was mostly charred rubble. He rode past the mill he'd spent five years building, past the once-grand house where he had brought his wife on their wedding night.

"Mr. Vigil?" The voice was masculine and, given that Jake knew most everybody in town, flat-out unfamiliar.

He turned in the saddle, saw a fussy-looking little man standing nearby, wearing a dusty suit and a bowler hat. "Ace Thompson," he said, extending one hand. Jake had already leaned down to accept the handshake before Thompson went on; otherwise, he probably would have kept his distance. "I'm with the railroad."

Jake swung a leg over the bay's neck and jumped down to face his visitor. Hands resting on his hips, he sighed. "Well, Mr. Thompson, it would seem that you and I are both out of luck. There's no timber and no place to mill it, anyhow. I reckon you could take my house, but that's gone, too." He folded his arms. "I'll be damned if I can come up with a solution."

Thompson looked surprised. "Well, it's true that you've suffered some serious losses here," he said. "No one is denying that. But we have the timber rights we acquired from your wife, and we'd like to lay tracks between here and Virginia City. If you'll agree to cut and plane the ties, we'll finance new equipment—"

Jake frowned. "Wait a minute," he interrupted. "Whoa. What do you mean, you have the timber rights *you acquired from my wife?*"

The other man blinked behind smudged spectacles. He wrenched them off, breathed on the lenses, and polished them vigorously with a corner of his handkerchief. "We certainly assumed you knew."

"Well," Jake growled, barely able to refrain from grabbing the little fellow by the lapels and yanking him up onto the toes of his boots, "I didn't. What the hell are you talking about?"

"Mrs. Vigil—your wife—offered to sell us whatever timber we needed."

The implications of what had actually happened struck Jake with a physical impact. How could she have done such a thing? How could she have done business with these vipers behind his back?

Thompson cleared his throat, and his glasses, Jake noticed, were still smudged. "Mrs. Vigil?" he prompted weakly.

"I know her name," Jake snapped. He was reeling inwardly. How could Skye have deceived him like this? She'd refused his offer to buy her surplus timber before they were married and then gone behind his back as soon as she had a ring on her finger and sold the logging rights out from under him. He was hot with betrayal, frantic to see his bride and demand an explanation. All the time she'd pretended to love him, she'd been planning his downfall.

"I'm sorry," said the little man. "It would seem that you were not apprised of your wife's intentions. However, I'm afraid we must insist that the deal be honored."

Jake turned away, groped for the bay, and swung up into the saddle. "Your bargain is with my wife," he said. "I won't interfere."

Thompson pushed the bowler hat to the back of his head and looked up. The sun blazed off the lenses of his spectacles, and he tugged at the hem of his suit coat with small, nervous hands. "I have more to tell you," he said.

"Sorry," Jake responded with a bitter smile. "I don't have time to listen." With that, he was gone, riding out of town.

Two hours later, he arrived at Fort Grant, and apparently the guards had seen him coming a long way off, for the towering, spiked timber gates swung open at his approach. Skye was waiting for him when he rode through, her head high, her chin out, and her eyes shining.

At the sight of him, she burst into tears. "Thank God," he heard her say, through the thrum that had filled his ears since he'd learned what she had done. "Thank God!"

He dismounted, approached her slowly. "You're all right, then, you and the boy?" he asked. A young soldier came, took the bay's reins, and led the animal away to be watered, fed, and groomed.

She nodded and dashed at her wet face with the back of one hand. She looked as though she wanted to fling herself into his arms, but she didn't. She just stood there, as if she'd been frozen, watching him. Consuming him with her eyes.

"Trace and Zachary are both fine," he said when he saw both Bridget and Christy coming toward him.

"Your mill?" Skye managed. "The house?"

"Gone," Jake said, careful to keep his distance.

Christy and Bridget reached them, and he nodded a greeting, told them their homes and husbands were safe. Relieved but obviously still very concerned about Skye, they returned to the barracks, casting anxious glances back over their shoulders as they went.

"Oh, Jake," Skye whispered. "I'm so sorry."

How he wanted to hold her, and be held by her, but he didn't dare let himself be taken in again. She was a liar, no better than Amanda; she'd sold him out for God only knew what reason, maybe spite, maybe just the sport of it. He'd thought she was so different, and he'd clearly been wrong. Well, he was a lousy judge of women, he'd proven that to his own satisfaction, and the best he could do was cut his losses and run.

"There's a Mr. Thompson in town looking for you," he said, as coolly as if he were speaking to a stranger. "He's with the railroad. Says you sold them your timber."

She swallowed, blinked once. Sniffled. She nodded again. "That's true. When you wouldn't accept it, I—"

He held up one hand. "Stop," he said. "I don't want to hear anything more."

She braced up and took a step toward him. "Well, you're going to listen to me all the same, Jake Vigil!" she exclaimed.

Jake looked nervously around, saw that life at Fort Grant was going on pretty much as usual. Soldiers were drilling, guards were patrolling the parapets, a small detachment was preparing to ride, probably headed up to Primrose Creek to relieve the troops already there. "What is there to say?" he hissed. "You

tricked me, and by God, I won't take that from anybody. Especially not my own wife!"

She had her hands on her hips by then, and there
was an obstinate snap in her eyes. "You're leaving
something out," she retorted fiercely. "After we were
married, I offered to *give* you all the timber you
needed. And you turned me down! Jake, don't you
see, I had to do something to keep the railroad from
moving in and taking——"

He moved in until his nose was less than an inch
from hers. "Enough!" he growled. "I won't hear any
of your excuses!"

"You were about to lose everything you had, everything you'd worked for! The money from the sale to
the railroad——"

"*Damn* the railroad *and* its money! I would have
thought of something!"

Out of the corner of one eye, Jake saw a flash of
pale hair and a bit of blue calico. "If you two want to
have a showdown," said Bridget Qualtrough, with
what amounted to towering dignity though she was
a small woman, "that's certainly your business. But
perhaps you wouldn't mind fighting it out in private?"

Skye reddened, and Jake felt a little ashamed himself, even though he was still convinced that he was
right. He stood there, his breath coming in deep, furious gasps, and tried to calm down. That took a while,
and when he thought he could trust himself not to
commence bellowing again, he took his wife loosely
by the elbow and, after a moment's assessment of their

surroundings, hustled her toward the chapel. Bridget, having made her intercession on behalf of the McQuarry family honor, retreated, but only so far as the wooden sidewalk, where she watched them with narrowed eyes, reminding Jake of a mother hen braced to defend a wayward chick.

The small church was blessedly empty, though the door was open to a spring freeze, and Jake seated Skye on a rear pew before sitting down beside her. Maybe it was the place, maybe it was that he'd had a chance to collect the scattered fragments of his temper, but Jake felt steadier and infinitely sadder.

"I've got nothing left to offer you," he said gruffly. "No trust. No house, no business, no money."

She touched his arm, though tentatively. "We have each other," she said. "We have Hank. And we have the land at Primrose Creek. We'll build a house and a barn and start over."

He merely shook his head.

"What about Hank?" she asked in a wretched whisper. "I promised him I'd be his mother."

"He can spend as much time with you as he wants." Jake thrust a hand through his hair and gazed at the stone floor of the little chapel, despondent.

"This is wrong," she said.

He laced his fingers together, looked briefly at the plain wooden cross affixed to the wall behind the rough-hewn pulpit. "I'm not sure how I'm going to manage it, but I will get another mill up and running, and when that happens, you and I will have a proper divorce. I'll see that you're provided for."

"I don't want your money!" she cried. She seemed to be simmering, like a pot forgotten on a hot stove, ready to rattle its lid. "Jake Vigil, you're a damn fool. I'm your wife. I'm trying to be a mother to Hank. My place is beside you, no matter what."

"You lied."

"I *didn't* lie. I simply failed to tell you——"

He held up a hand to silence her. "Please," he said. "No more."

She subsided then and sat still beside him, tears slipping down her cheeks, teeth sunk into her lower lip in what was probably an effort to regain control.

He stood. "I'd best go and speak to the boy," he said.

She didn't answer.

Before he left the chapel, he bent and kissed the top of her head in what they both knew was a gesture of farewell.

It was hard enough losing Jake. Losing Hank was beyond difficult. As little time as they'd managed to spend together, Skye and the boy had formed a bond, and parting was like tearing off skin.

They faced each other the next morning, woman and child, just inside the gates of Fort Grant. Jake had already loaded the wagon and climbed aboard; he was staring straight ahead, waiting for his son to join him. Together, they'd make a life that excluded Skye.

"I figure you would have made a pretty good ma," Hank said.

Skye's throat ached, and tears throbbed behind her eyes. "I'd like to go on being your friend, if that's all right with you," she managed to say. Then, with a sniffle, she rubbed her cheek with the heel of one palm.

Hank took a manful step forward and extended his little hand, as if to seal the bargain. "Friends," he said.

Skye nodded. She wanted to sweep Hank up in her arms and hold him close, if only for a moment, but she knew such a public display would embarrass him, so she didn't. "Look after your father," she said, just as he would have turned to hurry away toward the wagon.

Hank rolled his eyes in a way that might have been comical if Skye hadn't had a broken heart to deal with just then. "I don't see how I'm going to get much else done," he told her. With that, he turned and ran off to scramble up over the tailgate of Jake's wagon, nimble as a monkey.

Jake was watching Skye, and as he released the brake lever with one booted foot, he lifted a hand. Too soon, they'd be gone, out of sight.

Skye supposed she ought to wave back, but the truth was, she didn't have the strength to do even that much. So she just stood there, dying inside, hands locked together behind her back, looking on as the only man she had ever loved, the only man she ever *would* love, drove himself and his son right out of her life.

When the gates finally closed behind that

wagon, shutting Skye off from all her dreams, Bridget stepped up beside her and slipped an arm around her waist. She and Bridget had things to settle—the matter of the McQuarry secret, primarily—but just then she needed her sister. What would she have done, through all the difficulties, without Bridget?

"Come along," Bridget said gently. "I'm afraid there's something else we need to talk about."

Skye felt a swift rush of dread.

Bridget pulled her close against her side for a moment. "Megan's gone."

Skye stared. "What?"

"A freight wagon left the fort this morning for Virginia City, supposedly empty except for several canvas tarps. We think Megan was hiding under them."

"But surely she wouldn't do something like that—worry us this way—"

Bridget was steering her toward the barracks. "She left a note," she said. "Christy's in a state, and even Caney's all het up. We've got to put our heads together and work out what to do."

In the end, there was nothing they could do. Megan had left without knowing that the four of them were sisters, not cousins. According to her letter, she would be a famous stage actress before her next birthday. Skye was to keep the mare, Speckles, until she sent for it.

"Perhaps Zachary and Trace could find her," Bridget said.

Christy straightened her spine and shook her head. Her baby, Joseph, was nursing at her breast, modestly covered by a shawl borrowed from Bridget. "She's a McQuarry," she said. "We have to let her go. If we're lucky, she'll find her way back to us when she's ready."

7

~~~

"I don't much like livin' at the saloon," Hank told Skye. "That's why I spend so much time out here." They were sitting side-by-side on a log, facing Primrose Creek, fishing for trout. It had been a month since the fire, and the small community was, if anything, more active than ever before. The railroad had brought in a crew of its own to harvest trees on Skye's land, and, according to Trace, Jake had secured a loan from somewhere and bought a new steam-powered saw, which ran at full tilt, day and night, filling the air with the screech of progress and the lingering scent of sawdust.

There had been no word from Megan.

Skye squinted against the bright sunlight winking on the moving surface of the creek and brought her mind back to the idea of Jake and Hank living above Primrose Creek's one remaining saloon. That, she decided, was just plain ironic. Neither Skye, Bridget, nor Christy had any inclination to approach their mother, although Caney wasn't so reticent.

"I've got a thing or two I want to say to that woman," she'd announced after a conference on the matter.

Bridget, in the meantime, had advised Skye not to chase after Jake but to let him work things through in his own mind. She'd promised that he'd come to his senses in good time and realize that even if she had bungled things terribly, she'd only been trying to help him. So far, though, he showed no signs of doing so, and Skye hated knowing that her husband slept in that place every night. It was no comfort whatsoever that he theoretically shared quarters with his son, since Hank did indeed spend most of his time at Bridget and Trace's place, bunking in with Noah.

To complicate things further, Skye's monthly was late, and she suspected that she was carrying a child. In fact, she was certain of it. While she'd kept the news a secret from everyone so far, there would be no hiding the truth when five or six months had passed. Already, both Bridget and Caney were beginning to watch her, out of the corners of their eyes, as though they thought she would sprout something.

"I wish we could all live together, like we did before the fire," Hank said, and Skye realized how long she'd left the conversation hanging while she went woolgathering. She'd had a very difficult time concentrating on anything since her separation from Jake, though Megan's sudden flight worried her mightily. How *could* she have left without even saying good-bye?

And then there was Granddaddy's deception. It was almost more than a body could take in.

"I wish we could, too," she said sadly. Jake was an honorable man; he would probably insist on a reconciliation once he learned that he was going to be a father again, but she didn't want him to share her life out of a sense of obligation. And she was terribly afraid she wouldn't have the strength to refuse him, even on those terms, because she loved him so much. Her heart throbbed like a bad tooth; she couldn't eat, she couldn't sleep. All she could do was wait, it seemed. Wait and—following Caney's brisk advice to "make herself useful"—fish for rainbow trout.

"Pa asked me about you," Hank persisted. "Just this morning." A tug on his fishing line distracted him for a few moments, then he went on. "He said he hasn't seen you riding the bay stallion since you brought it back from Fort Grant, and he wondered if you'd sold it."

Skye's disappointment was abject—how like a man to be more concerned with a stallion than with his own wife—but she managed to hide her reaction because she got a fish on the line just then, a fat, gleaming trout, and it put up a respectable tussle before allowing itself to be caught. "You tell him I mean to breed the stallion to a few of Trace and Bridget's mares. Once they foal, I'll probably turn him loose. The stallion, I mean."

Hank was staring at her. "You'd do that? Let the stallion go? Let him be wild again?"

She smiled wistfully, baited her hook, and threw

her line back into the water. "Sure. He wasn't really mine. I just borrowed him for a while." She glanced behind her at the sprawling stands of timber, even now being thinned by the railroad's logging crew. "Sort of the way we borrow trees from the earth. If it's done right, the ones remaining thrive because they're getting more sunlight and water—more elbow room, you might say."

Hank's smile was bright and sudden. "We'll see him again, though, won't we? The bay?"

"Sure," Skye answered. "Every time we look at his colts and fillies, there he'll be, big as life." And every time she looked at her baby, she thought to herself, son or daughter, there Jake would be, in the child, looking back at her. The prospect was at once a joy and a sorrow.

In the near distance, Skye heard the sound of an approaching team and wagon, and she was grateful for the distraction. She drew in her line, set her pole aside, and turned, shading her eyes from the blazing summer sun, to watch as the rig came over the knoll into the meadow where she meant to build her house.

The wagon was drawn by six mules, and though Malcolm Hicks, Caney's beau, was at the reins, Jake Vigil rode along on the seat beside him.

Skye stood her ground, folded her arms, and waited as her estranged husband jumped down from the high wagon box and came striding toward her.

He didn't speak up right away but simply looked at her, revealing absolutely nothing of his feelings—if he had any. She couldn't rightly tell whether he did or not, since he generally guarded his emotions as fiercely as a troll guarded a bridge.

"What do you want?" she was finally forced to ask. She figured they'd still have been standing there when the snows came, staring at each other, if she hadn't broken the silence.

"I've missed you," Jake confessed, but he took his time about it. He hooked his thumbs under the snaps of his suspenders.

Skye was taken aback, afraid to hope that Bridget had been right, that the wait was over and Jake Vigil had at last realized where he belonged. With her and with Hank, right here on the banks of Primrose Creek.

She gestured weakly toward the wagon, where Mr. Hicks waited, one scarred but rapidly healing arm resting against his side. The rig was stacked high with freshly planed planks. "I didn't order any lumber."

Jake smiled. "Yes," he said, "you did. I just refused to sell it to you, remember?" He spotted his son, standing close by and listening intently. "Hullo, Hank. How about giving Malcolm a hand with the team?"

Fairly radiating curiosity, Hank obeyed. When he was out of earshot, Jake went on. "I haven't been able to think straight since we talked at Fort Grant," he began.

She put her hands on her hips. "Since *you* talked, you mean. You weren't doing much listening, as I recall."

He chuckled ruefully and shook his head. "No, I

guess I wasn't. The point is, I've tried living without you, and I've been just plain miserable every moment of that time. I think about you at night, and I think about you in the morning, and all the time in between. You're the woman I want to spend my life with—I guess I knew that way back when we danced that night at the Community Hall, though I couldn't bring myself to take the chance." He stopped, drew a deep breath, and let it out slowly. "I've done a lot of thinking these past few weeks, Mrs. Vigil. I never loved Amanda, and I never loved Christy, either. Fact is, I didn't know what love was until I met you. I'm asking you to give me another chance, Skye. It's that simple."

Skye's heart had swollen to fill her throat. Words were impossible, but tears sprang to her eyes, telling him far more than she would have chosen to reveal in an hour of talk.

Jake came near enough to take her shoulders in his big hands. "This is the first of the lumber we'll need to build our house," he said. "All you have to do is say it's all right for Hank and me to live here with you."

She swallowed painfully. "You mean—?"

He nodded. "Yes," he said. "If you'll have us."

She threw her arms around his neck, and he laughed aloud and spun her around in a dizzying circle before setting her on the ground again and kissing her soundly. When she surfaced, she heard Mr. Hicks and Hank cheering like spectators watching a sack race. She felt a little like cheering herself.

"I love you, Jake," she said, and her eyes filled again.

He brushed her mouth with his. "Thank God for that," he replied.

She took his hand, led him a little way down the creek bank, filled with sweet nervousness. "There's something I need to tell you."

He arched an eyebrow, and his expression was wary. "What?"

"You're going to be a father," she said. "Again."

"You're sure?" He nearly whispered the words.

"Pretty sure," she replied with a nod. She knew her body, knew its flows and rhythms, and there was a child growing inside her. Jake's child, and her own.

For a long moment, Jake just stood there, looking as though he'd been pole-axed. Then he let out such a shout of jubilation that Skye nearly lost her balance and fell right into the creek. He lifted her up again, this time putting one arm under her knees with the other supporting her back, and carried her up the bank and through the tall grass like a prize taken in battle.

"My wife," he told Malcolm and Hank in a voice that seemed to echo off the Sierras themselves, "is going to have a baby!"

Malcolm grinned at the announcement. Hank was beaming, and his little chest seemed to have expanded, he looked so puffed up. Skye remembered their conversation at Jake's, when she'd told him there would be babies coming and she'd need lots of help from him to look after them.

Jake kissed Skye's ear and set her gently on her feet. Then he walked over to Hank and sat on his haunches so that their eyes met, his and the boy's. "This is all right with you, isn't it?" he asked.

Hank's freckled face was shining. Since he'd come to Primrose Creek, he'd filled out considerably, and with every passing day he seemed to have more confidence in the future and in other people. No doubt, he was more certain of Jake than anybody else, which was as it should have been. "I'll teach him to spit," he said. "Unless he's a girl. Girls don't spit."

Jake chuckled and ruffled Hank's hair. "Well, most of them don't, anyway," he replied. He stood and turned to face Skye. "Now, Mrs. Vigil," he said, "perhaps you wouldn't mind telling us just where you'd like this house of ours to sit and all like that."

"I won't have a mansion," she warned. Her heart was singing, and if she hadn't been struggling so hard to hold on to her dignity, she would have danced around the meadow in great leaps of joy, with both arms outspread and her face raised to the blue, blue sky.

He laughed. "Don't worry," he said. "Right now, I couldn't afford a chicken coop, not on my own, anyhow."

"But you're willing to live here with me?" She could hardly believe her ears, even though this was just what Bridget had predicted, back at Fort Grant and several times since. And Bridget was right about most things, whether the rest of the family liked to admit it or not. "You and Hank?"

"I'm more than willing," Jake replied hoarsely, facing her again and cupping her elbows in his hands. "I love you," he repeated.

She knew her eyes were twinkling with mischief. "So you say, Mr. Vigil," she teased. "So you say. But I'm going to need proof."

He reddened delightfully, cleared his throat, and glanced back at Mr. Hicks and Hank, who were busy with the team and wagon. While Mr. Hicks began unloading lumber, whistling as he worked, Hank unhitched the horses and led them, one by one, down to the stream.

"Relax," Skye whispered, running the tip of one index finger down the front of his shirt, bumping over each button. "I can wait until tonight. But no longer than that, Mr. Vigil. Not one minute longer than that."

He laughed. "I'm persuaded, Mrs. Vigil," he replied. And then he kissed her again.

One month later
Room 11, the Comstock Hotel
Virginia City, Nevada

"You can't seriously expect to hear anything," Skye said when Jake laid his head on her bare belly. "It's far too early."

He planted a smacking kiss where his ear had been, eliciting a reluctant, croonlike groan from his bride. Although they'd been married two months by that time, they had just managed to get away for a honeymoon. They'd arrived in Virginia City that afternoon by wagon, and so far they hadn't even been outside the room to eat.

"When our baby makes a sound, I want to be there to hear it," Jake said, sitting up in the well-rumpled linens of the bed. They were just across the street from Virginia City's famous Opera House, and Jake had promised they would see at least one performance before they went home to Primrose Creek.

So far, it seemed to Skye, they'd been the ones doing all the performing, she and Jake. The strange thing was, every time they made love, it was better than the time before; it didn't seem possible, but there it was.

Skye stretched languidly and wound a finger in a lock of Jake's hair. She hoped their daughters would have his hair; her own was straight as a yardstick. "This baby will make plenty of sounds after she's born," she said. "Are you going to be there to hear that, too?"

He laughed. "Of course," he said. "When I'm not busy providing for my wife and growing family, that is." Mischievously, he began kissing her belly again.

Skye whimpered. "Jake——"

"Mmmm?"

She trembled. "I'm hungry, and you promised to take me to the Opera House."

He ran the tip of his tongue along a strategic path. "So I did. And I will. After——"

"Not after," she said, but already her breath was quickening and her hips were rising and falling in that old, all-too-familiar rhythm. "Now."

"After," he murmured.

Skye gasped. "After," she cried.

*   *   *

They had steaks for dinner in the hotel's fancy dining room and then crossed the busy, rutted street to the Opera House. According to the bill posted beside the ticket booth, there was an orchestra on hand to accompany a famous soprano named Nellie Baker. While Skye had never heard of the woman, she was delighted to be there nonetheless.

Inside, they found and took their seats, programs in hand. The interior of the theater was anything but rustic; the place was awash in gilt and velvet, and there were brass reflectors behind the gas footlights and paintings right on the walls themselves, just like the frescoes in Italy.

Skye was practically giddy with happiness—first the long, poignantly passionate hours alone with Jake in their room, then that delicious dinner, and now an evening of culture. At least, that was what Christy called it. Christy loved living at Primrose Creek as much as any of them, but she did tend to bemoan the lack of "genteel pursuits."

Skye was wearing a special dress, a lightweight red wool with black velvet at the collar and cuffs, made just for her and just for this occasion by Bridget and Caney. She was carrying a child, and the man she loved was beside her, loving her back. She hadn't known it was possible to have so much and wondered if it might be dangerous. Might anger the fates—

Jake must have been watching her face, for he took her chin lightly between his thumb and forefinger and scolded. "What's this? Did I see a shadow in those beautiful eyes, just for a moment there?"

She smiled, and the seats around them continued to fill with all manner of fascinating people, saddle bums and millionaires, saints and sinners, matrons and fancy women. "I was hoping we might see Megan," she admitted. "Do you think she's already moved on?"

He brushed her forehead with his lips. "Maybe."

"She doesn't know—"

He smoothed a tendril of hair against her temple. "She'll come back when she's ready, Skye," he said. "You have to believe that."

She sighed and nodded.

He touched the tip of her nose. The gesture was an intimate one—they might have been alone, for the way it affected Skye—and infinitely tender. "Things always change," he reminded her quietly. "We'll make it, though. The whole lot of us—McQuarrys and Qualtroughs, Shaws and Vigils."

The gaslights went down just then, but Skye continued to gaze at her husband, and she knew her eyes were shining. "I love you so much," she said.

"You're just saying that because you mean it," he replied.

The orchestra tuned up, and then the soprano came onstage, a tall, rotund woman, drenched in feathers and beads. She sang for an hour, and although Skye had heard better voices in the church choir, her gaze barely strayed from the woman throughout the evening. For all her bulk and for all her shortcomings as a singer, Nellie Baker conveyed high emotion in even the smallest gesture, and by the time she got to her closing number, a forlorn and sentimental song about a poor granny on the rocky shores of Ireland, vainly watching the sea for the return of her fishermen sons and grandsons, Skye was reduced to tears.

Jake handed Skye his handkerchief, and she dabbed delicately at her eyes, while the grizzled miner in the other seat blew his nose loudly into a bandanna plucked from his shirt pocket.

"That was *lovely*," Skye sighed when the applause had ended and the lights were turned up again. "Do you think she knows Megan? The two of them being in show business and all?"

Jake grinned, raised her hand to his mouth, and kissed her knuckles. Then he laughed and pulled her to her feet. "Come on, Mrs. Vigil. We'll go backstage and ask. Then we'll take ourselves a walk in the moonlight."

No one in the cast of that evening's production knew of anyone named Megan McQuarry, and though Skye was disappointed, she wasn't surprised. For all she knew, her cousin—sister—had changed her name.

Skye and Jake made their way outside, through the crowds of vociferous theatergoers. Opinions simmered in the air and mingled with tinny piano music from the many saloons.

Skye and Jake walked away from the main street, where gambling houses and brothels, hotels, and other such places dominated, down a hill, and into a churchyard. From there, they could look out over the rough, bare grandeur of the valley. Virginia City itself had sprung up virtually overnight when the Comstock Lode was discovered; there was no timber for miles. Had it not been for the tons of high-grade silver buried quite literally beneath the streets of the town, it was doubtful that anyone would have chosen to settle there.

Skye was having a wonderful time, more than wonderful, but she would be glad to get back to Primrose Creek, back to the trees and the stream, the sizable cabin Jake had built, mostly with his own hands. Trace and Zachary had helped a great deal, of course, and so had Malcolm Hicks, but it was Jake who worked far into the night, time after time, even after a full day at the mill.

He interlocked his fingers with hers and kissed the knuckles. "I'm glad we don't live here," he said.

She laughed. "I was just thinking along those same lines."

"We can go home tomorrow, if that's what you want." He pulled her gently against him and kissed the top of her head. He smelled of good tobacco, soap, and that unique scent that was his alone.

She looked up at him. "You hated that soprano," she accused, but she was smiling.

"Not personally." He grinned. "I wasn't that crazy about her voice, it's true, but I'm willing to undergo any sort of torture if it makes you happy. Such is my love for my bride."

She rolled her eyes. "Her voice wasn't that bad. That last song was very touching."

"That last song was stupid," he said. Skye was discovering that Jake said what he thought most times, straight out. She didn't mind, though; she was used to the McQuarrys.

He smoothed a tendril of hair back from her forehead. "Did you enjoy yourself tonight?" he asked with a tenderness that made her heart soar out over the valley like a bird taking wing. "That's all that really matters."

"I enjoyed myself," she said, cocking her head to one side, and touched the cleft in his chin with a fingertip. "But I'd rather enjoy you."

He laughed aloud, and kissed her smartly. "Insatiable wench," he said.

"I've never denied it," she replied, and he laughed again.

They turned and saw the lights of Virginia City looming above them. Then, arm-in-arm, they began the climb together.

Also available from

Linda Lael Miller

The Bestselling
Springwater Seasons Series:

Springwater

•

Rachel

•

Savannah

•

Miranda

•

Jessica

•

A Springwater Christmas

POCKET BOOKS

SONNET
BOOKS

2398